SHADOWS OF SEVILLE An
Artistic Mystery Romance

Adela Vesper

Published by Palette of Intrigue, 2024.

SHADOWS OF SEVILLE AN ARTISTIC MYSTERY ROMANCE

First edition. June 24, 2024.

Copyright © 2024 Adela Vesper.

ISBN: 979-8227926845

Written by Adela Vesper.

Also by Adela Vesper

Palette of Intrigue - A Female-Led Mystery Unveiling Barcelona Art
Scene
Echoes of Wycliffe : A Legacy Restored
The Lady's Secret : A Regency Affair
SHADOWS OF SEVILLE An Artistic Mystery Romance

Chapter 1: Arrival in Sevilla

Mia Valdés stepped off the train and onto the platform at Sevilla-Santa Justa station, taking a moment to breathe in the warm, fragrant air of southern Spain. The sun was already high, casting golden light over the ancient city. She adjusted her bag over her shoulder and took in the sight before her—Sevilla, a city known for its rich history, vibrant culture, and now, her next big art exhibition.

The trip from Barcelona had been long but restful, giving Mia plenty of time to reflect on her career. This exhibition was a significant milestone, a chance to showcase her work to a broader audience and to further cement her reputation in the art world. Her mind buzzed with anticipation and a touch of nervousness.

Mia's dark hair, tied back in a loose bun, was slightly tousled from the journey. Her attire—simple yet elegant, with a touch of bohemian flair—reflected her artistic nature. She hailed a taxi, her excitement bubbling over as she directed the driver to her hotel. The drive through the city was a sensory feast; the narrow, winding streets of the old town, the grandeur of the cathedral, and the scent of orange blossoms in the air all left her in awe.

The taxi arrived at her hotel, a charming boutique establishment in the heart of the city. Mia checked in, her eyes wide with admiration at the traditional Andalusian decor. The hotel's inner courtyard, with its mosaic tiles and serene fountain, provided a peaceful retreat from the bustling city outside. She quickly freshened up in her room, eager to explore the city before meeting with Alejandro, the gallery owner hosting her exhibition.

Mia set out on foot, her first stop being the gallery. The streets of Sevilla were alive with activity, from street performers to bustling cafes. She found herself enchanted by the city's energy, her artist's eye constantly catching new details—the play of light on the river, the intricate ironwork of the balconies, the vibrant colors of the buildings.

The gallery was situated in a beautiful old building, its facade adorned with intricate carvings and large windows that hinted at the treasures within. Mia stepped inside, greeted by the cool, air-conditioned air and the soft murmur of voices. The gallery was already a hive of activity, with staff making final preparations for the exhibition.

"Mia Valdés, welcome to Sevilla!" A deep, resonant voice drew her attention. She turned to see Alejandro Martín, the gallery owner, striding towards her. Alejandro was a tall man in his early fifties, with salt-and-pepper hair and a commanding presence. His eyes, sharp and discerning, missed nothing.

"Alejandro, it's a pleasure to finally meet you in person," Mia replied, extending her hand.

Alejandro shook her hand warmly. "The pleasure is mine. I've been looking forward to this exhibition for months. Your work has generated quite the buzz."

Mia smiled, feeling a mix of pride and humility. "I'm thrilled to be here. Sevilla is such an inspiring city."

Alejandro led her through the gallery, giving her a tour of the space where her paintings would soon be displayed. The gallery was spacious and well-lit, with high ceilings and an elegant, minimalist design that allowed the art to take center stage. Mia could already envision her pieces hanging on the walls, each one a testament to her journey as an artist.

As they walked, Alejandro shared stories about the local art scene, introducing her to some of the staff and a few artists who were there finalizing their own exhibits. It was a tight-knit community, and Mia felt welcomed.

Later that afternoon, as Mia was making final adjustments to her displays, she noticed a man across the gallery, intently studying one of her paintings. He was tall and lean, with tousled dark hair and an air of quiet intensity. He wore a casual yet stylish outfit, and a camera hung from a strap around his neck, identifying him as a photographer.

Intrigued, Mia approached him. "Hello, I'm Mia Valdés," she said, extending her hand.

The man looked up, his dark eyes meeting hers. He smiled warmly and took her hand. "Ivan Morales. It's a pleasure to meet you, Mia. Your work is truly captivating."

"Thank you, Ivan. Are you here for the exhibition?" she asked, curious about his presence.

"Yes, I am. I'm a photographer, and I've been documenting the art scene in Sevilla for a project. Your work caught my eye," Ivan explained, his gaze returning to the painting he had been studying.

Mia felt a spark of connection. "What do you find most interesting about it?" she asked, genuinely curious.

Ivan considered her question for a moment. "I love the way you play with light and shadow, the depth of emotion in your brushstrokes. It's as if each painting tells a story, inviting the viewer to look closer, to delve deeper."

Mia felt a flush of pleasure at his words. "That's exactly what I aim for. Art should evoke a response, draw people in."

Ivan nodded, his smile widening. "You've certainly succeeded. I'd love to hear more about your inspiration and your process, if you have the time."

Mia glanced at her watch, realizing that she had a few hours free before the evening's events. "I'd love that. How about we grab a coffee and chat?"

Ivan agreed, and they left the gallery together, walking through the sun-dappled streets of Sevilla. They found a cozy cafe with outdoor seating, and as they sipped their drinks, they talked about art, travel, and life. Mia found Ivan to be not only charming but also deeply insightful, his perspective as a photographer offering a fresh angle on her own work.

As the afternoon turned into evening, Mia felt a growing sense of connection with Ivan. There was an ease in their conversation, a shared passion for creativity that bridged any gaps between them. By the time they returned to the gallery for the evening's events, Mia felt as though she had known Ivan for much longer than just a few hours.

The gallery was buzzing with excitement as guests began to arrive for the pre-exhibition reception. Mia mingled with the crowd, feeling a mixture of nerves and exhilaration. She introduced Ivan to several of the other artists and patrons, and it was clear that his charm and genuine interest in their work made a positive impression.

As the evening progressed, Alejandro called for attention, making a short speech to officially open the exhibition. He spoke eloquently about the significance of the event, highlighting the unique contributions of each artist. When he introduced Mia, she felt a surge of pride and gratitude, stepping forward to acknowledge the applause.

Mia's exhibition was a resounding success. Her paintings drew praise from critics and collectors alike, and she found herself caught up in a whirlwind of conversations and congratulations. Ivan stayed by her side for much of the evening, their easy camaraderie drawing curious glances from those around them.

By the end of the night, Mia felt both exhilarated and exhausted. She stepped outside to catch her breath, the cool night air a welcome relief from the bustling gallery. Ivan joined her, and they stood together in comfortable silence for a moment.

"Congratulations, Mia. Tonight was a triumph," Ivan said, his voice warm with genuine admiration.

"Thank you, Ivan. I couldn't have asked for a better reception," Mia replied, her heart full.

They stood there for a few more moments, the connection between them palpable. Mia felt a flutter of anticipation, wondering where this newfound bond with Ivan might lead. As she looked out over the beautiful city of Sevilla, she knew that this was just the beginning of a new chapter in her life—one filled with promise, creativity, and perhaps, a touch of romance.

Chapter 2: The Exhibition

The morning sun filtered through the delicate lace curtains of Mia's hotel room, casting intricate patterns on the floor. She stretched luxuriously in bed, the excitement of the previous night still buzzing through her veins. Today was the official opening of her exhibition, and she felt a mix of nerves and exhilaration. The night before had been a resounding success, but today's events would be the true test of her work's impact on Sevilla's art scene.

After a quick breakfast, Mia made her way to the gallery. The streets of Sevilla were already bustling with life, the air filled with the scent of freshly baked bread and the sound of chatter and laughter. She felt a deep sense of connection to the city, its vibrant energy mirroring her own creative spirit.

Upon arriving at the gallery, Mia was greeted by Alejandro, who looked as dapper as ever. His sharp eyes sparkled with anticipation. "Mia, good morning! I trust you're ready for the big day?"

"Absolutely, Alejandro. Last night was incredible, and I'm eager to see how today unfolds," Mia replied, her smile reflecting her excitement.

The gallery staff was already hard at work, making final adjustments to the displays and ensuring everything was perfect for the influx of visitors. Mia took a moment to walk through the gallery, her eyes lingering on each of her paintings. She felt a surge of pride seeing her work in such a prestigious setting, knowing that it had resonated with so many people.

As the doors opened to the public, the gallery quickly filled with art enthusiasts, critics, and collectors. Mia found herself engaged in countless conversations, each one reinforcing her belief in the power of art to connect and inspire. She moved from one group to another, answering questions about her techniques, her inspirations, and the stories behind her paintings.

In the midst of the crowd, Mia spotted Ivan. He stood out with his casual yet stylish attire, his camera slung over his shoulder. Their eyes met, and he made his way towards her, a warm smile spreading across his face.

"Good morning, Mia. Ready for another exciting day?" Ivan greeted her, his voice carrying a hint of flirtation.

"Good morning, Ivan. Absolutely. I'm thrilled to see so many people here," Mia replied, her heart skipping a beat at his charming demeanor.

"I can see why. Your work is stunning, and it clearly resonates with people," Ivan said, his eyes locking onto hers with an intensity that made her blush.

They continued to talk, their conversation flowing effortlessly. Ivan's interest in her work was genuine, and Mia found herself opening up to him about her creative process and the personal experiences that had shaped her art. Their connection deepened with each passing moment, the chemistry between them palpable.

As the day went on, Ivan took numerous photographs, capturing the essence of the exhibition and the reactions of the visitors. Mia admired his skill and the way he seemed to find beauty in even the smallest details. She felt a growing attraction to him, drawn not just to his charm and good looks, but also to his passion for his craft.

In the early afternoon, there was a scheduled press conference, and Mia found herself standing before a throng of reporters and cameras. Alejandro introduced her, speaking eloquently about her contributions to the art world and the significance of her exhibition in Sevilla. Mia took a deep breath and stepped forward, ready to address the crowd.

"Thank you, Alejandro, and thank you all for being here today. It's an incredible honor to share my work with you," Mia began, her voice steady despite her nerves. "Art has always been a way for me to express my deepest emotions and to connect with others on a profound level.

This exhibition represents not just my journey as an artist, but also the stories and experiences that have shaped me."

She continued to speak, her words flowing with passion and sincerity. The reporters listened intently, their questions probing but respectful. Mia felt a sense of accomplishment as she addressed each one, confident in her ability to articulate the meaning and purpose behind her art.

After the press conference, Mia was approached by several prominent figures in the art world. One of them was Isabella, a renowned art collector with a reputation for discovering emerging talent. She was an elegant woman in her late fifties, with a discerning eye and an air of sophistication.

"Mia, your work is truly exceptional. I've been following your career for some time, and I'm very impressed," Isabella said, her voice smooth and cultured.

"Thank you, Isabella. That means a lot coming from you," Mia replied, feeling a mixture of pride and humility.

"I'd like to discuss the possibility of adding some of your pieces to my collection. Perhaps we could arrange a meeting later this week?" Isabella suggested, her eyes twinkling with genuine interest.

"I'd be delighted. Let's set a time that works for both of us," Mia agreed, thrilled at the prospect of having her work featured in such a prestigious collection.

As the afternoon wore on, Mia and Ivan found a quiet corner of the gallery to talk. The crowd had thinned out slightly, giving them a chance to catch their breath and reflect on the day's events.

"You were amazing up there, Mia. Your speech was inspiring," Ivan said, his admiration evident.

"Thank you, Ivan. It's been such a whirlwind, but in the best way possible," Mia replied, her eyes shining with excitement.

"I have to ask, what's your next big project? I'm sure everyone is dying to know what you'll do next," Ivan asked, his curiosity piqued.

Mia thought for a moment, a smile playing on her lips. "I have a few ideas brewing. I've been exploring themes of transformation and renewal, and I think my next series will delve into those concepts. But I'm also open to where inspiration takes me."

"That sounds fascinating. I'd love to document your process, if you'd be open to it. There's something magical about capturing an artist at work," Ivan suggested, his eyes lighting up with excitement.

"I'd love that, Ivan. Your photography is incredible, and I think it would add a new dimension to my work," Mia replied, feeling a flutter of excitement at the prospect of collaborating with him.

Their conversation was interrupted by Alejandro, who approached with a smile. "Mia, there's someone I'd like you to meet. He's a major player in the art world and very interested in your work."

Mia excused herself and followed Alejandro, her heart racing with anticipation. She was introduced to Carlos, a prominent art critic known for his insightful reviews and influential opinions. They engaged in a lively discussion about her work, and Mia was thrilled to receive his praise and encouragement.

As the day drew to a close, Mia felt a sense of fulfillment and joy. The exhibition had been a resounding success, and she had made valuable connections with influential figures in the art world. But more than that, she had found a kindred spirit in Ivan, whose passion and creativity matched her own.

The gallery began to empty out as the evening approached, and Mia found herself alone with Ivan once more. They stood together, looking at one of her favorite paintings—a piece that depicted a stormy sea gradually giving way to calm waters.

"This one speaks to me," Ivan said softly, his eyes fixed on the painting. "It's like a metaphor for life's struggles and the peace that comes after."

"That's exactly what I was trying to convey," Mia replied, touched by his understanding. "It's one of my favorites too."

They stood in silence for a moment, the connection between them growing stronger. Mia felt a surge of emotions, a mix of excitement, attraction, and a deep sense of camaraderie. She turned to Ivan, her eyes meeting his.

"Thank you for being here, Ivan. It's meant a lot to me," Mia said, her voice filled with sincerity.

"I wouldn't have missed it for the world, Mia. Your art is incredible, but it's your passion and spirit that truly inspire me," Ivan replied, his gaze unwavering.

As they stood together in the dimly lit gallery, the spark between them ignited into a flame. Mia felt a warmth spread through her, a sense of possibility and hope. She knew that this was just the beginning of something beautiful—both in her career and in her connection with Ivan.

The exhibition had not only showcased her work but had also opened doors to new opportunities and relationships. As Mia and Ivan walked out of the gallery into the cool night air, she felt a sense of gratitude and excitement for the future. Sevilla had welcomed her with open arms, and she was ready to embrace all that the city and her new life had to offer.

Chapter 3: The Gallery Owner

The morning sun bathed Sevilla in a warm, golden light, casting long shadows across the cobblestone streets. Mia woke early, the events of the previous day still fresh in her mind. The exhibition had been an overwhelming success, and she was eager to see what new opportunities would unfold today. She dressed quickly, opting for a comfortable yet stylish outfit that reflected her artistic sensibilities, and made her way to the gallery.

As she entered the gallery, Mia was greeted by the sight of staff bustling about, preparing for another busy day. The energy in the air was palpable, a mix of anticipation and excitement. Alejandro was already there, overseeing the preparations with his usual commanding presence. He spotted Mia and walked over, a warm smile on his face.

"Good morning, Mia. I trust you slept well?" Alejandro greeted her, his voice rich and resonant.

"Good morning, Alejandro. Yes, I did, thank you. Yesterday was incredible, and I'm looking forward to today," Mia replied, her eyes bright with enthusiasm.

Alejandro nodded, his expression thoughtful. "I'm glad to hear that. There's someone I'd like you to meet. He's a significant figure in the art world and has been very supportive of our gallery. I think you'll find him quite interesting."

Mia's curiosity was piqued. "I'd love to meet him. Who is he?"

Alejandro gestured towards a figure standing at the far end of the gallery, examining one of Mia's paintings. "That's Rafael Ortega. He's a well-known art critic and collector. His reviews can make or break an artist's career, and he has a keen eye for talent."

Mia felt a flutter of nerves. Meeting Rafael Ortega could be a turning point in her career. She took a deep breath and followed Alejandro across the gallery. As they approached, Rafael turned to face them, his sharp eyes appraising her with interest.

"Rafael, I'd like you to meet Mia Valdés, the artist behind these remarkable works," Alejandro introduced her, his tone respectful.

"Mia, it's a pleasure to meet you. I've heard a lot about your work, and I must say, seeing it in person has been a revelation," Rafael said, extending his hand.

Mia shook his hand, her nerves easing slightly at his kind words. "Thank you, Mr. Ortega. I'm honored to have your interest."

"Please, call me Rafael. I'd love to hear more about your inspiration and your creative process," Rafael said, his gaze intense but friendly.

As they talked, Mia found herself opening up about her journey as an artist, the challenges she had faced, and the experiences that had shaped her work. Rafael listened attentively, his questions thoughtful and insightful. It was clear that he had a deep understanding and appreciation for art, and Mia felt a connection with him, akin to the bond she had felt with Ivan.

After their conversation, Rafael excused himself to continue exploring the gallery. Alejandro turned to Mia, his eyes twinkling with satisfaction. "You made quite an impression on him. Rafael is not easily impressed, but I could see he was genuinely interested in your work."

"Thank you, Alejandro. It was a pleasure to meet him," Mia replied, feeling a sense of accomplishment.

As the day went on, Mia continued to engage with visitors, answering questions and sharing stories about her paintings. The gallery was filled with a diverse crowd, from seasoned art collectors to young enthusiasts, all captivated by the vibrant energy of the exhibition.

In the early afternoon, Mia noticed Ivan entering the gallery, his camera in hand. He made his way towards her, his smile warm and genuine. "Hello, Mia. How's everything going?"

"Ivan, it's great to see you. Everything's been wonderful. I met Rafael Ortega earlier, and he was very complimentary about my work," Mia said, her excitement evident.

"I'm not surprised. Your art speaks for itself," Ivan replied, his eyes sparkling with admiration. "I was wondering if you'd like to take a break and grab some lunch. There's a fantastic little café nearby that I think you'd love."

Mia hesitated for a moment, glancing around the gallery. But the prospect of spending more time with Ivan was too tempting to resist. "That sounds lovely. Let me just let Alejandro know."

After a quick word with Alejandro, who encouraged her to take a break, Mia joined Ivan, and they walked to the café. The streets of Sevilla were lively, the air filled with the sounds of street musicians and the aroma of delicious food. The café Ivan had mentioned was a charming spot with outdoor seating and a view of a bustling plaza.

They found a table and ordered their meals, the conversation flowing easily between them. Mia felt a deepening connection with Ivan, their shared passion for art and creativity forming a strong bond.

As they enjoyed their lunch, Ivan asked, "So, what's next for you, Mia? Do you have any upcoming projects or exhibitions?"

"I have a few ideas I'm working on, but nothing concrete yet. I'd love to explore more themes of transformation and renewal in my next series. And, of course, I'm open to new opportunities," Mia replied, her mind buzzing with possibilities.

"I'd love to document your process, if you're open to it. There's something magical about capturing an artist at work, and I think it would add a new dimension to your art," Ivan suggested, his eyes lighting up with excitement.

Mia felt a thrill at the idea. "I'd love that, Ivan. Your photography is incredible, and I think it would be a wonderful collaboration."

As they talked, Mia realized how much she enjoyed Ivan's company. His insights and perspectives were refreshing, and she felt inspired by his passion and creativity. By the time they returned to the gallery, she knew that this was the beginning of a beautiful friendship, and possibly something more.

Back at the gallery, Mia resumed her role as hostess, engaging with visitors and sharing her love for art. Ivan continued to take photographs, capturing candid moments and the vibrant energy of the exhibition.

Later in the afternoon, Alejandro approached Mia with a thoughtful expression. "Mia, there's something I need to discuss with you. It's about Alejandro, the gallery owner."

Mia's curiosity was piqued. "What is it?"

"There have been some tensions among the local artists. Alejandro has always been a bit of a mystery, and there are rumors that he's involved in some questionable dealings. I've heard whispers of financial discrepancies and rivalries that have caused friction in the art community," Alejandro explained, his tone serious.

Mia felt a pang of concern. She had sensed an underlying tension among the artists, but she hadn't realized the extent of it. "Do you think it could affect the exhibition?"

"It's hard to say. Alejandro is influential, and his support has been crucial to many artists, but these rumors could tarnish his reputation and the gallery's," Alejandro replied.

Mia nodded, her mind racing with thoughts. She had always admired Alejandro's dedication to promoting art, but the possibility of his involvement in dubious activities was troubling. She decided to keep an eye out for any further signs of trouble, determined to protect her work and the integrity of the exhibition.

As the day drew to a close, Mia felt a mix of emotions. The exhibition had been a resounding success, and she had made valuable connections with influential figures in the art world. But the shadows of doubt and tension lingered, casting a pall over her triumph.

That evening, Mia joined Ivan and a few other artists for a casual dinner at a local tapas bar. The atmosphere was lively, the conversation animated and filled with laughter. Mia felt a sense of camaraderie and belonging, grateful for the friendships she had formed.

As they walked back to their hotels, Ivan turned to Mia, his expression serious. "Mia, I want you to know that I'm here for you. If there's anything you need, whether it's for your art or dealing with the tensions at the gallery, you can count on me."

Mia felt a warmth spread through her at his words. "Thank you, Ivan. That means a lot to me. I'm glad we met."

They said goodnight, and Mia returned to her hotel room, her mind buzzing with the events of the day. As she lay in bed, she couldn't help but think about the challenges ahead. The art world was a complex and sometimes treacherous place, but she was determined to navigate it with integrity and passion.

Mia drifted off to sleep, her dreams filled with images of her paintings, the vibrant streets of Sevilla, and the faces of the people she had met. She knew that this was just the beginning of her journey, and she was ready to face whatever came next with courage and creativity.

Chapter 4: A Night Out

Mia awoke to the soft sounds of Sevilla coming to life outside her window. The gentle murmur of the city was a comforting backdrop as she stretched and prepared for another day. Her thoughts drifted to the previous evening, her conversations with Ivan, and Alejandro's warnings about the tensions in the art community. There was a lot to process, but for now, she had a day filled with promise ahead of her.

After a quick breakfast, Mia headed back to the gallery. She spent the morning mingling with visitors, sharing stories behind her paintings, and soaking in the positive feedback. The energy in the gallery was palpable, and Mia felt a profound sense of fulfillment as she watched people connect with her work.

Around midday, Ivan arrived, his camera ready as always. He captured candid moments of Mia interacting with guests and the intricate details of her artwork. Whenever their eyes met, Mia felt a flutter of excitement, their growing bond adding a new layer of enjoyment to the exhibition.

As the afternoon turned to evening, the gallery began to quiet down. Ivan approached Mia, a playful glint in his eye. "How about we take a break and explore the city? There's so much more to Sevilla than just the gallery."

Mia smiled, feeling a thrill of anticipation. "I'd love that. Where should we start?"

"I have a few places in mind," Ivan replied, his voice filled with enthusiasm. "Let's start with a stroll along the Guadalquivir River."

They left the gallery and headed towards the river, the evening light casting a golden glow over the city. The streets were alive with people enjoying the cool evening air, and the atmosphere was vibrant and relaxed. As they walked, Ivan pointed out various landmarks, sharing bits of history and personal anecdotes that made Mia appreciate the city even more.

They reached the river and followed the path along its edge. The water shimmered in the fading light, and the gentle breeze carried the scent of orange blossoms. Mia felt a sense of peace wash over her, the worries of the day melting away.

"So, Mia," Ivan began, breaking the comfortable silence, "what do you love most about being an artist?"

Mia thought for a moment, her eyes on the water. "I think it's the freedom to express myself, to convey emotions and stories through my work. Art has always been a way for me to make sense of the world and to connect with others. There's something incredibly powerful about creating something that resonates with people on a deep level."

Ivan nodded, his expression thoughtful. "I feel the same way about photography. It's about capturing moments, telling stories through images. There's a magic in freezing a moment in time, in seeing the world from a different perspective."

They continued to walk, their conversation flowing effortlessly. Mia found herself opening up to Ivan in a way she hadn't with anyone in a long time. His passion for his craft, his insights, and his genuine curiosity about her work made her feel seen and understood.

As the sky darkened, they decided to find a place for dinner. Ivan led Mia to a charming tapas bar tucked away in a quiet corner of the city. The bar was cozy and inviting, with warm lighting and a lively atmosphere. They found a table and ordered a variety of dishes, eager to sample the local cuisine.

Over plates of patatas bravas, jamón ibérico, and gambas al ajillo, Mia and Ivan continued to talk, their connection growing deeper with each passing moment. They shared stories of their travels, their creative journeys, and their hopes for the future. Mia felt a warmth spread through her, a sense of belonging that she hadn't felt in a long time.

After dinner, they wandered through the narrow streets of the old town, the buildings illuminated by soft, golden lights. The sound of flamenco music drifted from a nearby bar, adding to the enchanting ambiance. Ivan suggested they stop in to watch a performance, and Mia eagerly agreed.

The bar was small and intimate, with a stage set up for the musicians and dancers. They found seats near the front, and Mia felt a thrill of excitement as the performers took the stage. The music was passionate and soulful, the dancers' movements a mesmerizing blend of grace and intensity. Mia was captivated, the raw emotion of the performance resonating deeply with her.

As the night drew on, Mia and Ivan found themselves lost in the magic of the city. They explored hidden alleyways, stumbled upon quaint little shops, and laughed together at the quirky surprises Sevilla had to offer. The bond between them grew stronger, the chemistry undeniable.

At one point, they found themselves in a quiet square, the only sounds the distant hum of the city and their own laughter. Ivan turned to Mia, his expression serious but his eyes filled with warmth. "Mia, I've really enjoyed spending time with you tonight. There's something about you that's incredibly inspiring."

Mia felt her heart race, a mix of excitement and nervousness. "I feel the same way, Ivan. I'm so glad we met."

They stood there for a moment, the air charged with unspoken possibilities. Ivan reached out and gently took Mia's hand, his touch sending a shiver down her spine. "I'd love to see more of your work, to understand what drives you as an artist. Maybe we could spend more time together, both here in Sevilla and beyond?"

Mia's heart swelled with emotion. "I'd like that, Ivan. I'd like that a lot."

They continued to walk, hand in hand, the night unfolding around them like a beautiful, intricate tapestry. Mia felt a sense of hope and excitement for the future, knowing that this was just the beginning of something special.

As they made their way back to the hotel, Ivan walked Mia to her door. He hesitated for a moment, then leaned in and placed a gentle kiss on her cheek. "Goodnight, Mia. I'll see you tomorrow."

"Goodnight, Ivan. Thank you for a wonderful evening," Mia replied, her cheeks flushed with warmth.

She watched as Ivan walked away, a smile on her lips and her heart full. As she entered her room and closed the door behind her, Mia felt a sense of contentment and anticipation. Sevilla had already brought so much into her life, and she couldn't wait to see what the future held.

Lying in bed, Mia replayed the evening in her mind, her thoughts filled with Ivan's smile, the magic of the city, and the promise of new beginnings. She knew that the path ahead might be uncertain, but with Ivan by her side, she felt ready to face whatever challenges came her way.

As sleep finally claimed her, Mia dreamed of vibrant colors, swirling patterns, and the boundless possibilities of her art and her newfound connection with Ivan. The journey was just beginning, and she was eager to embrace it with open arms and an open heart.

Chapter 5: The Murder

The morning sun streamed through the windows of Mia's hotel room, bathing everything in a soft, golden light. She stretched lazily, a smile playing on her lips as she remembered the wonderful night she had spent with Ivan. The magic of Sevilla had worked its charm, and she felt more inspired and alive than she had in a long time.

Mia dressed quickly, eager to get to the gallery and continue sharing her art with the world. She opted for a flowing dress that matched her mood—light, vibrant, and full of promise. As she walked through the bustling streets, the city seemed even more beautiful in the morning light, each corner revealing new wonders and hidden gems.

Upon arriving at the gallery, Mia noticed an unusual stillness in the air. The staff, usually bustling about with energy and purpose, were gathered in small groups, whispering among themselves. There was a palpable tension, and Mia felt a chill run down her spine.

"Mia, over here!" Alejandro's voice cut through the murmur of the crowd. He was standing near the entrance, his expression grave.

Mia hurried over, her heart pounding with unease. "Alejandro, what's going on?"

Alejandro's face was pale, his eyes filled with concern. "It's Alejandro, the gallery owner. He... he's been found dead."

The words hit Mia like a physical blow, and she felt the ground shift beneath her feet. "What? How?"

"It appears he was found early this morning in his office. The police are treating it as suspicious," Alejandro explained, his voice shaking slightly.

Mia's mind raced as she tried to process the news. Alejandro, the man who had welcomed her to Sevilla, who had believed in her work, was gone. The gallery, once a haven of creativity and inspiration, now felt tainted by tragedy.

"I can't believe it," Mia whispered, her voice barely audible. "Do they have any idea what happened?"

"Not yet. The police are conducting a thorough investigation. They've already questioned some of the staff, and they'll want to speak with you too," Alejandro said, his expression somber.

Mia nodded, her thoughts a whirlwind of confusion and sorrow. She made her way to the gallery office, where a few police officers were already at work, collecting evidence and interviewing staff. The atmosphere was tense, the usual vibrancy of the gallery replaced by a somber silence.

Inspector Ruiz, a stern-looking man with sharp features, approached Mia. "Miss Valdés, I understand you were one of the last people to see Alejandro alive. I'd like to ask you a few questions."

Mia took a deep breath, steadying herself. "Of course, Inspector. I'll do anything I can to help."

They moved to a quieter corner of the gallery, and Inspector Ruiz began his questioning. "Can you tell me about your interactions with Alejandro yesterday?"

Mia recounted her conversations with Alejandro, detailing the events of the day. She explained how she had met with Rafael Ortega, engaged with visitors, and discussed the exhibition's success. As she spoke, she couldn't help but remember Alejandro's warning about the tensions among the local artists.

"Did Alejandro mention anything unusual or seem concerned about anything specific?" Inspector Ruiz asked, his eyes fixed on Mia.

"He did mention some tensions in the art community," Mia replied, choosing her words carefully. "He said there were rumors of financial discrepancies and rivalries that had caused friction among the artists."

Inspector Ruiz made a note of her statement. "Did he mention any names or specific incidents?"

"No, he didn't go into details. He just seemed worried about the impact it might have on the gallery," Mia said, her mind racing to remember every detail of their conversation.

The inspector nodded, his expression thoughtful. "Thank you, Miss Valdés. We'll be in touch if we have any further questions. In the meantime, please stay available and let us know if you remember anything else."

Mia nodded, feeling a sense of helplessness wash over her. She watched as the police continued their work, the gravity of the situation sinking in. Alejandro's death was a devastating loss, and the implications for the gallery and the art community were profound.

As the day wore on, Mia tried to focus on her work, but her thoughts kept drifting back to Alejandro. She couldn't shake the feeling that there was more to his death than met the eye. The gallery felt different now, a shadow hanging over its once-bright atmosphere.

In the early afternoon, Ivan arrived at the gallery, his expression serious. He had heard the news and came to offer his support. "Mia, are you okay? I heard about Alejandro."

Mia felt a wave of relief at his presence. "I'm trying to process it all. It's just so sudden and tragic."

Ivan took her hand, his touch comforting. "I'm here for you. Whatever you need."

They sat together in a quiet corner of the gallery, talking about Alejandro and the impact he had on their lives. Mia felt a sense of solace in Ivan's company, his steady presence a balm to her troubled mind.

As the afternoon turned to evening, the police finished their initial investigation and left the gallery. The staff began to clean up, trying to restore some sense of normalcy. Mia knew that things would never be the same, but she was determined to honor Alejandro's memory by continuing to share her art and inspire others.

That evening, Ivan suggested they take a walk to clear their minds. They wandered through the streets of Sevilla, the city's beauty a stark contrast to the darkness they felt. As they walked, Ivan shared stories of his own experiences with loss and how he had found strength in his art.

Mia felt a deepening connection with Ivan, his empathy and understanding drawing her closer. They talked late into the night, their bond growing stronger with each shared moment.

By the time they returned to Mia's hotel, she felt a sense of clarity. She knew that she couldn't let Alejandro's death overshadow the exhibition or her work. She had to find a way to move forward, to continue creating and inspiring, even in the face of tragedy.

Before saying goodnight, Ivan turned to Mia, his expression serious but filled with warmth. "Mia, I know this is a difficult time, but I believe in you. You have the strength to get through this, and I'm here to support you every step of the way."

Mia felt a surge of gratitude and affection for Ivan. "Thank you, Ivan. Your support means everything to me."

As she lay in bed that night, Mia thought about the road ahead. The investigation into Alejandro's death was just beginning, and she knew there would be challenges and uncertainties. But she also knew that with Ivan by her side, she could face whatever came her way.

Mia drifted off to sleep, her dreams filled with images of her art, the vibrant streets of Sevilla, and the faces of those she had come to care for. She was ready to embrace the future, no matter how uncertain, with courage and creativity.

Chapter 6: The Investigation Begins

The next morning, Mia woke to the soft glow of the sunrise filtering through her hotel room window. The events of the previous day weighed heavily on her mind. Alejandro's sudden death had cast a long shadow over the exhibition, and the uncertainty of the situation left her feeling uneasy. Determined to face the challenges ahead, she dressed quickly and made her way to the gallery.

Upon arriving, Mia was met with a subdued atmosphere. The staff, still reeling from the shock, moved about with quiet determination, trying to keep the gallery running smoothly. Mia offered them encouraging smiles, knowing that they needed reassurance as much as she did.

Inspector Ruiz was already at the gallery, speaking with Alejandro, the gallery manager, and a few other key staff members. His presence, though necessary, only served to heighten the tension in the air. Mia approached him, hoping to gain some clarity on the situation.

"Inspector Ruiz, good morning. Have there been any new developments?" Mia asked, trying to keep her voice steady.

Ruiz looked up from his notes, his expression serious. "Good morning, Miss Valdés. We're still in the early stages of the investigation, but I wanted to speak with you again. There are a few more questions I need to ask."

Mia nodded, feeling a knot of anxiety tighten in her stomach. "Of course. Whatever I can do to help."

They moved to a quiet corner of the gallery, away from the prying eyes and ears of the staff and visitors. Ruiz took out his notepad and began his questioning.

"Miss Valdés, can you think of anyone who might have had a motive to harm Alejandro? Any rivalries or conflicts that you're aware of?" Ruiz asked, his eyes fixed on Mia.

Mia thought carefully, recalling Alejandro's words about the tensions among the local artists. "Alejandro mentioned some tensions and rivalries, but he didn't give me any specifics. He did seem concerned about financial discrepancies and the impact they could have on the gallery."

Ruiz made a note of her response. "Did Alejandro ever mention any specific artists or individuals he was worried about?"

Mia shook her head. "No, he didn't. But I did get the sense that he was trying to protect the gallery and its reputation."

The inspector nodded, his expression thoughtful. "Thank you, Miss Valdés. We're following up on several leads, and your information is helpful. If you think of anything else, no matter how small, please let me know."

"I will, Inspector. Thank you," Mia replied, feeling a mixture of relief and concern.

As Ruiz moved on to speak with other staff members, Mia made her way through the gallery, her mind racing with thoughts of Alejandro and the possible suspects. She couldn't shake the feeling that there was more to the story, and she was determined to uncover the truth.

In the afternoon, Ivan arrived at the gallery, his presence a welcome comfort. He greeted Mia with a warm hug, his eyes filled with concern. "How are you holding up, Mia?"

"I'm managing, Ivan. It's been a lot to process, but I'm trying to stay focused," Mia replied, grateful for his support.

"I've been thinking about Alejandro's death. There's something about it that doesn't sit right with me," Ivan said, his voice low.

"What do you mean?" Mia asked, her curiosity piqued.

"I've been doing some research, talking to people in the art community. There are whispers of financial troubles and shady dealings. I think Alejandro might have been involved in something bigger than we realized," Ivan explained, his expression serious.

Mia felt a chill run down her spine. "Do you think his death could be connected to these dealings?"

"It's possible. I don't want to jump to conclusions, but there are too many coincidences to ignore," Ivan replied.

They decided to start their own investigation, determined to uncover the truth. Ivan suggested they begin by looking into Alejandro's recent activities and the people he had been in contact with. Mia agreed, feeling a renewed sense of purpose.

Their first stop was Alejandro's office, which had been sealed off by the police. With some persuasion, they managed to get permission from Inspector Ruiz to review Alejandro's records. The office was a treasure trove of information, with files and documents detailing the gallery's operations and Alejandro's interactions with artists and collectors.

As they sifted through the paperwork, Mia noticed a series of emails that caught her attention. They were from a wealthy art collector named Isabella, discussing various transactions and acquisitions. The tone of the emails was friendly but hinted at a deeper, more complicated relationship.

"Look at this, Ivan," Mia said, pointing to the screen. "These emails from Isabella. They seem... unusual."

Ivan leaned over to read the emails, his brow furrowing. "You're right. There's something off about them. We should definitely look into her."

They made a note to investigate Isabella further, hoping to uncover any connections she might have had with Alejandro's death. As they continued their search, Mia found another intriguing piece of information—a ledger detailing financial transactions that seemed inconsistent with the gallery's official records.

"This ledger doesn't match up with the gallery's accounts. There are large sums of money being moved around, but it's not clear where it's coming from or where it's going," Mia said, her voice tinged with suspicion.

Ivan nodded, his expression grim. "It looks like Alejandro was involved in some kind of financial scheme. We need to find out who else was involved and what they were trying to achieve."

As they delved deeper into the records, Mia and Ivan began to piece together a complex web of financial dealings and personal relationships. It became clear that Alejandro's death was not an isolated incident but part of a larger, more sinister plot.

By the time they left the office, Mia felt both exhausted and invigorated. They had uncovered crucial information, but there was still much work to be done. She knew that they were getting closer to the truth, but the journey ahead was fraught with danger and uncertainty.

That evening, Mia and Ivan decided to take a break and clear their minds. They found a quiet café near the gallery and settled in with cups of coffee, their conversation turning to lighter topics. Despite the gravity of the situation, Mia felt a sense of camaraderie and hope. With Ivan by her side, she knew they could face whatever challenges lay ahead.

As they walked back to their hotels, Ivan took Mia's hand, his touch reassuring. "Mia, I know this is difficult, but we're making progress. We'll find out what happened to Alejandro and bring those responsible to justice."

Mia squeezed his hand, her heart swelling with gratitude. "Thank you, Ivan. I couldn't do this without you."

They said goodnight, and Mia returned to her hotel room, her mind buzzing with thoughts of the investigation. She knew that the road ahead would be challenging, but she was ready to face it with determination and courage.

Lying in bed, Mia thought about the people she had met in Sevilla, the connections she had formed, and the journey she had embarked on.

She was determined to honor Alejandro's memory by uncovering the truth and continuing to create art that inspired and connected people.

As sleep finally claimed her, Mia dreamed of vibrant colors, swirling patterns, and the boundless possibilities of her art and her investigation. The journey was just beginning, and she was ready to embrace it with open arms and an open heart.

Chapter 7: Clues and Conflicts

The sun was just beginning to rise over Sevilla when Mia awoke, the first light of dawn casting a soft glow through her hotel window. She stretched and got out of bed, her mind already racing with thoughts of the investigation. Alejandro's death had left a void in the art community, and Mia felt a deep responsibility to uncover the truth.

After a quick breakfast, Mia headed to the gallery, her steps purposeful and determined. She had agreed to meet Ivan there to continue their investigation into Alejandro's mysterious dealings. The streets were quieter than usual, the city still waking up, and Mia appreciated the calm before the day's events unfolded.

When she arrived at the gallery, Ivan was already there, waiting for her. He greeted her with a warm smile and a quick hug. "Morning, Mia. Ready to dig deeper?"

"Absolutely. I couldn't sleep much last night, thinking about everything we've uncovered," Mia replied, her eyes reflecting her determination.

They headed to Alejandro's office, which had been left untouched since their last visit. The room was a maze of papers, files, and personal items, each one potentially holding a clue to the mystery they were trying to solve.

Mia and Ivan started by going through the emails they had found the day before. They focused on the correspondence between Alejandro and Isabella, hoping to uncover more about their relationship and any potential conflicts. As they read through the messages, a pattern began to emerge—Isabella had been pushing Alejandro to make certain acquisitions and deals that seemed unusual and potentially risky.

"Ivan, look at this," Mia said, pointing to an email dated a few weeks before Alejandro's death. "Isabella was insisting that Alejandro purchase a series of paintings from a relatively unknown artist. She mentioned that the deal had to be done quickly and discreetly."

Ivan leaned over to read the email, his brow furrowing. "That does seem strange. Why would Isabella be so insistent on this particular deal? And why the urgency?"

Mia nodded, her mind racing with possibilities. "It's almost as if she was trying to hide something. We need to find out more about this artist and the paintings."

They made a note of the artist's name and continued their search. As they sifted through more emails and documents, they came across another intriguing piece of information—a series of bank transfers between Alejandro's account and an offshore account linked to Isabella.

"These transfers are huge," Ivan said, his voice filled with concern. "Alejandro was moving a lot of money, and it's all linked to Isabella. This definitely points to something shady."

Mia agreed, feeling a growing sense of urgency. "We need to follow the money. If we can trace these transfers, we might be able to uncover the full extent of their dealings."

With a clearer picture forming, Mia and Ivan decided to take their findings to Inspector Ruiz. They knew that the police had more resources and could potentially access information that was beyond their reach.

At the police station, Inspector Ruiz listened intently as Mia and Ivan presented their evidence. His expression grew more serious with each new piece of information.

"Thank you for bringing this to my attention," Ruiz said, his tone grave. "This confirms some of our own suspicions, and it gives us a clearer direction for the investigation. We'll need to follow up on these bank transfers and look into this artist Isabella was so interested in."

Mia felt a sense of relief, knowing that they were making progress. "Please keep us informed, Inspector. We want to help in any way we can."

Ruiz nodded. "I appreciate your cooperation, Miss Valdés. This case is complex, and your insights are invaluable. We'll be in touch."

Leaving the police station, Mia and Ivan felt a renewed sense of purpose. They had taken a significant step forward, but there were still many unanswered questions.

As they walked through the streets of Sevilla, Ivan suggested they take a break and grab some lunch. They found a quiet café and settled into a corner table, their conversation turning to lighter topics as they enjoyed their meal. Despite the seriousness of their investigation, Mia felt a sense of comfort in Ivan's presence. His support and understanding were a source of strength for her.

After lunch, they decided to visit the artist whose paintings Isabella had been so insistent on acquiring. The artist, Luis Ramirez, had a small studio in a less touristy part of the city. Mia hoped that meeting him might shed some light on the mysterious deal.

They arrived at the studio and knocked on the door. After a moment, it was opened by a young man with tousled hair and paint-splattered clothes. He looked at them with curiosity. "Can I help you?"

"Hello, are you Luis Ramirez?" Mia asked, offering a friendly smile.

"Yes, that's me. Who are you?" Luis replied, his eyes flicking between Mia and Ivan.

"I'm Mia Valdés, an artist, and this is Ivan Morales, a photographer. We're investigating the recent death of Alejandro, the gallery owner. We found some correspondence suggesting he was planning to purchase several of your paintings. We were hoping you could tell us more about that," Mia explained.

Luis's expression darkened at the mention of Alejandro's death. "I heard about that. It's terrible. Alejandro had been in touch with me about buying some of my work, but the deal fell through before anything was finalized."

"Do you know why Isabella was so interested in your paintings?" Ivan asked, his tone gentle but probing.

Luis shook his head, a puzzled look on his face. "Not really. I was just happy that someone of her stature was interested in my work. It would have been a big break for me."

Mia and Ivan exchanged a glance, their suspicions growing. "Did Alejandro mention why the deal didn't go through?" Mia asked.

"He seemed worried about something, but he didn't go into details. Just said that he couldn't go through with the purchase," Luis replied, his voice tinged with frustration.

They thanked Luis for his time and left the studio, their minds buzzing with new questions. It was clear that there was more to the story, and they were determined to uncover the truth.

As they walked back through the city, Ivan turned to Mia, his expression thoughtful. "We're getting closer, Mia. I can feel it. We just need to keep digging."

Mia nodded, her resolve strengthening. "We will. Alejandro deserves justice, and we need to find out what Isabella is hiding."

That evening, they returned to Mia's hotel to review their findings and plan their next steps. They spread out the documents and notes they had collected, trying to piece together the puzzle.

As they worked, Mia felt a growing sense of connection with Ivan. Their shared determination and passion for uncovering the truth had brought them closer together, and she found herself relying on his strength and support more than ever.

"Thank you, Ivan," Mia said, her voice soft. "I couldn't do this without you."

Ivan looked at her, his eyes filled with warmth. "We're in this together, Mia. We'll find the truth, no matter what it takes."

They continued to work late into the night, their bond growing stronger with each passing moment. Mia knew that the road ahead would be challenging, but with Ivan by her side, she felt ready to face whatever came their way.

As they finally called it a night and Ivan prepared to leave, he paused at the door, turning back to Mia. "Stay safe, Mia. We're getting closer, but that also means it's getting more dangerous."

Mia nodded, her heart full of gratitude and determination. "You too, Ivan. We'll get through this together."

With a final smile, Ivan left, and Mia settled into bed, her mind racing with thoughts of the investigation and the deepening bond she felt with Ivan. She knew that the journey ahead would be difficult, but she was ready to face it with courage and creativity.

As sleep finally claimed her, Mia dreamed of vibrant colors, swirling patterns, and the boundless possibilities of her art and her investigation. The journey was just beginning, and she was ready to embrace it with open arms and an open heart.

Chapter 8: Uncovering Secrets

The first rays of the morning sun illuminated Mia's room as she awoke, feeling a sense of determination coursing through her veins. Today was a new day, and she was resolute in her quest to uncover the truth behind Alejandro's death. After a quick breakfast, she met Ivan at the gallery, their expressions mirroring each other's resolve.

"Good morning, Mia," Ivan greeted her, his eyes filled with a mixture of warmth and seriousness. "Ready to dive back into the investigation?"

"Absolutely," Mia replied, her voice steady. "We need to find out more about Isabella and her connection to Alejandro. There's something she's hiding, and we need to uncover it."

They decided to start by visiting the places Alejandro had frequented in the days leading up to his death. Their first stop was a high-end café known to be a popular spot among the art community. They hoped to find someone who might have seen or heard something useful.

The café was bustling with activity, filled with artists, collectors, and critics engaged in lively conversations. Mia and Ivan took a seat at a corner table, their eyes scanning the room for familiar faces. They didn't have to wait long before a young waitress approached them, a friendly smile on her face.

"Good morning. What can I get for you?" she asked, her notepad ready.

"Two coffees, please," Mia replied, her mind already focused on the next steps. "And if you have a moment, we'd like to ask you a few questions about Alejandro, the gallery owner."

The waitress's smile faded slightly, replaced by a look of curiosity and concern. "I heard about what happened. It's terrible. Alejandro was a regular here. What do you need to know?"

"We're trying to piece together his last few days," Ivan explained. "Did you notice anything unusual about his behavior recently? Any meetings or conversations that stood out?"

The waitress thought for a moment, her brow furrowing. "Well, he did meet with a woman a few times. They seemed to be discussing something serious. She was very elegant, probably in her late fifties. I remember because she had this distinctive, expensive-looking bracelet."

Mia and Ivan exchanged a knowing glance. "Did you happen to hear what they were talking about?" Mia asked, her tone gentle.

The waitress shook her head. "I didn't catch much, but they seemed tense. It wasn't a friendly chat, more like a negotiation or an argument."

"Thank you, that's very helpful," Ivan said, his voice sincere. "If you remember anything else, please let us know."

They finished their coffees and left the café, their minds buzzing with new information. The description of the woman matched Isabella perfectly, and the tense meetings suggested that their relationship was more complicated than it seemed.

Their next stop was a nearby park where Alejandro often went for walks. They hoped to find someone who might have seen him there. As they walked through the lush greenery, Mia felt a sense of tranquility, the beauty of the surroundings a stark contrast to the turmoil of their investigation.

Near a bench shaded by a large oak tree, they spotted an elderly man feeding pigeons. He looked up as they approached, his eyes sharp and inquisitive.

"Good morning," Mia greeted him with a smile. "We're looking into the recent death of Alejandro, the gallery owner. We were told he often came here. Did you happen to see him recently?"

The man nodded, his expression thoughtful. "Alejandro was a good man. Always took the time to chat with me. Yes, I saw him a few days before he died. He seemed troubled, distracted. I asked him if everything was alright, but he just said he had a lot on his mind."

"Did he mention anything specific?" Ivan asked, his tone respectful.

"No, but he did say something about a deal he was working on. Said it was causing him a lot of stress," the man replied, his eyes filled with sadness.

"Thank you for your help," Mia said, feeling a pang of sorrow for Alejandro's struggles.

As they continued their walk through the park, Mia and Ivan discussed their findings. It was clear that Alejandro had been under significant pressure, likely related to the deals Isabella had been pushing.

"We need to find out more about these deals," Ivan said, his voice filled with determination. "Let's go back to the gallery and see if we can find any more records or correspondence."

Back at the gallery, they resumed their search in Alejandro's office. Mia focused on the financial records while Ivan combed through the emails and notes. After several hours of meticulous searching, they stumbled upon a folder hidden at the back of a drawer. Inside were documents detailing several art acquisitions and sales, many of which seemed suspicious.

"Look at this," Mia said, holding up a contract. "It's for the purchase of a series of paintings from Luis Ramirez. The terms are incredibly favorable for Luis, almost too good to be true."

Ivan examined the contract, his expression serious. "It's as if Alejandro was being forced to make these purchases. Maybe Isabella was using him to launder money or cover up illegal activities."

Mia felt a surge of determination. "We need to confront Isabella. If she's involved in something illegal, she needs to be held accountable."

They decided to visit Isabella's mansion, hoping to catch her off guard and get some answers. The drive to her estate was filled with a tense silence, both of them bracing for the confrontation ahead.

Isabella's mansion was an imposing structure, surrounded by meticulously manicured gardens. As they approached the front door, Mia felt a sense of foreboding. They rang the doorbell, and after a few moments, Isabella herself answered, her expression a mixture of surprise and irritation.

"Mia, Ivan, what are you doing here?" she asked, her voice cold.

"We need to talk, Isabella," Mia said, her tone firm. "It's about Alejandro."

Isabella's eyes narrowed, but she stepped aside to let them in. They followed her into a lavish sitting room, the opulence of the surroundings in stark contrast to the tension in the air.

"What is it you want to know?" Isabella asked, her voice sharp.

"We found some suspicious documents in Alejandro's office," Ivan said, not mincing words. "Contracts and financial records that suggest you were pressuring him into questionable deals. We need to know the truth, Isabella."

Isabella's face hardened, her eyes flashing with anger. "You have no right to accuse me of anything. Alejandro was a friend, and I would never do anything to harm him."

"We have evidence, Isabella," Mia said, her voice steady but insistent. "Bank transfers, emails, contracts. It's clear that something was going on, and we need to understand what it was."

Isabella stood up, her posture rigid. "I have nothing more to say. Leave now, before I call the police."

Mia and Ivan exchanged a glance, knowing they had pushed as far as they could for now. They left the mansion, feeling a mixture of frustration and determination.

As they drove back to the city, Ivan spoke, his voice filled with resolve. "Isabella is hiding something. We need to find out what it is and expose her."

Mia nodded, her mind racing with thoughts of their next steps. "We'll keep digging. We'll find the truth, Ivan."

That evening, they met with Inspector Ruiz again, sharing their findings and the tense encounter with Isabella. Ruiz listened carefully, his expression growing more serious with each new piece of information.

"Thank you for your diligence," Ruiz said, his tone respectful. "We'll follow up on these leads and see what we can uncover about Isabella's dealings. In the meantime, stay safe. This investigation is becoming more dangerous."

Mia and Ivan agreed, feeling the weight of the inspector's words. As they left the police station, they knew that the stakes were higher than ever. They were getting closer to the truth, but the path ahead was fraught with danger.

That night, as Mia lay in bed, she felt a mixture of exhaustion and determination. The investigation was uncovering more secrets than she had anticipated, and she knew that the journey was far from over. But with Ivan by her side, she felt a sense of strength and hope.

As sleep finally claimed her, Mia dreamed of vibrant colors, swirling patterns, and the boundless possibilities of her art and her investigation. The journey was just beginning, and she was ready to embrace it with open arms and an open heart.

Chapter 9: The Collector

The next morning dawned bright and clear, casting a golden light over the city of Sevilla. Mia awoke feeling a mix of exhaustion and determination. The events of the past days had taken their toll, but she knew they were on the verge of uncovering something significant. Today, they would investigate Isabella further and try to understand the full extent of her involvement.

After a quick breakfast, Mia met Ivan at the gallery. He looked as determined as she felt, and they exchanged a quick hug before diving back into their investigation.

"I've been thinking about Isabella," Ivan said as they walked through the gallery. "She's a powerful figure in the art world, and she has the means to cover her tracks. We need to be smart about how we approach this."

Mia nodded. "I agree. We need to find someone who knows her well, someone who might have seen or heard something that can give us more insight into her dealings with Alejandro."

They decided to start by visiting a few prominent figures in the art community who might have had interactions with Isabella. Their first stop was the home of Carlos Herrera, a respected art critic and collector who had attended Mia's exhibition. They hoped he might have some information that could help them.

Carlos lived in a beautiful townhouse in one of Sevilla's historic neighborhoods. As they approached the door, Mia felt a sense of anticipation. They rang the bell, and after a few moments, Carlos himself opened the door, his expression curious.

"Mia, Ivan, what a surprise," Carlos greeted them warmly. "What brings you to my home?"

"We need to talk to you about Isabella," Mia said, getting straight to the point. "We believe she was involved in Alejandro's death, and we're trying to uncover the truth."

Carlos's expression grew serious, and he invited them inside. They followed him to a cozy sitting room, where he offered them coffee and listened as they explained their investigation.

"I knew Alejandro well," Carlos said, his voice thoughtful. "He was a good man, dedicated to his work. Isabella, on the other hand, has always been an enigma. She's charming and influential, but there have been whispers about her dealings for years."

"Do you know anything specific about her relationship with Alejandro?" Ivan asked, leaning forward.

Carlos hesitated for a moment, then nodded. "I know that Isabella was very interested in certain pieces of art that Alejandro was acquiring. She seemed to have a personal stake in those deals, and there were rumors that she was using him to launder money through the gallery."

Mia and Ivan exchanged a glance, their suspicions confirmed. "Do you have any idea why Alejandro would go along with it?" Mia asked.

Carlos sighed. "Alejandro was a passionate man, but he had his weaknesses. He was deeply in debt, and Isabella offered him a way out. She promised to help him financially if he agreed to her terms. It was a dangerous game, and I warned him about it, but he was desperate."

Mia felt a pang of sorrow for Alejandro. He had been caught in a web of deception, and it had ultimately cost him his life. "Do you think anyone else in the art community might have more information?"

Carlos thought for a moment. "There is someone who might know more—Isabella's personal assistant, Marta. She's been with Isabella for years and would have seen everything. If you can get her to talk, you might find the answers you're looking for."

They thanked Carlos for his help and left his home, their next destination clear. They needed to find Marta and convince her to share what she knew. It was a risky move, but they were running out of options.

After some searching, they discovered that Marta lived in a modest apartment on the outskirts of the city. They drove there, hoping she would be willing to talk. When they arrived, they found Marta in the small garden behind her building, tending to a patch of flowers. She looked up as they approached, her expression wary.

"Hello, Marta," Mia began, her voice gentle. "We're friends of Alejandro, and we're trying to find out what happened to him. Can we talk to you for a few minutes?"

Marta hesitated, then nodded slowly. "Alright. Come inside."

They followed her into the apartment, which was small but tidy, filled with personal touches that spoke of a simple, quiet life. Marta offered them tea and sat down, her eyes filled with a mixture of fear and determination.

"I've been expecting someone to come asking about Alejandro," Marta said quietly. "I didn't want to believe it, but I knew Isabella's dealings would catch up to her eventually."

Mia and Ivan listened intently as Marta began to share her story. She described how Isabella had manipulated Alejandro, using his financial troubles to control him and push through her own agendas. She spoke of secret meetings, suspicious transactions, and the growing tension between Isabella and Alejandro.

"Isabella was ruthless," Marta said, her voice trembling. "She would do anything to get what she wanted. Alejandro tried to break free, but she threatened him. She said she would ruin him if he didn't comply."

"Do you know anything about the specific deals they were involved in?" Ivan asked.

Marta nodded. "There were several, but the most significant was the purchase of those paintings from Luis Ramirez. Isabella wanted them for reasons I never fully understood. There was something valuable about them, something she was willing to go to great lengths to obtain."

Mia felt a chill run down her spine. The pieces of the puzzle were starting to come together, but there were still so many unanswered questions. "Do you know why those paintings were so important to her?"

Marta shook her head. "No, but I overheard something once. Isabella mentioned a hidden message or code in the paintings, something that could lead to a fortune. I thought it was just a story, but now I'm not so sure."

Mia and Ivan exchanged a glance, their minds racing with possibilities. If Isabella believed there was something valuable hidden in the paintings, it explained her obsession with acquiring them. They needed to get a closer look at those artworks.

"Thank you, Marta," Mia said, her voice filled with gratitude. "You've been a great help. We'll take it from here."

As they left Marta's apartment, Mia felt a renewed sense of determination. They had uncovered crucial information, but there was still much to be done. They needed to find the paintings and decipher whatever message they held.

Their first step was to contact Luis Ramirez again. They arranged a meeting at his studio, hoping he could provide more insight into his work and the potential hidden message.

Luis greeted them warmly, his expression curious as they explained what they had learned. "I've heard rumors about hidden messages in art before, but I never imagined it would be in my own work," he said, his brow furrowing.

"Do you remember anything unusual about the paintings you sold to Alejandro?" Mia asked, her voice gentle but insistent.

Luis thought for a moment. "I did experiment with some new techniques in those pieces, using layers of paint and different textures. It's possible there's something hidden beneath the surface, but I never looked closely."

Mia and Ivan exchanged a determined glance. "Can we examine the paintings?" Ivan asked. "We need to see if we can uncover this hidden message."

Luis agreed, and they spent the next few hours carefully examining the artworks. Using a combination of ultraviolet light and careful scraping, they began to reveal hidden symbols and patterns beneath the layers of paint. It was slow, meticulous work, but the results were undeniable—there was something hidden in the paintings, something that Isabella had been desperate to obtain.

As the symbols and patterns emerged, Mia felt a sense of awe and excitement. They had uncovered a hidden code, one that might lead them to the truth about Alejandro's death and Isabella's schemes.

By the time they finished, it was late in the evening. They thanked Luis for his help and left the studio, their minds buzzing with the possibilities of what they had discovered.

"We need to decipher this code," Ivan said as they walked back to their car. "It's the key to everything."

Mia nodded, her eyes filled with determination. "We will. We're getting closer, Ivan. We're going to uncover the truth and bring justice for Alejandro."

That night, Mia and Ivan returned to Mia's hotel to work on deciphering the code. They spread out their notes and photos of the paintings, methodically analyzing each symbol and pattern. It was painstaking work, but they were driven by a sense of purpose and determination.

As the hours passed, they began to piece together the meaning of the code. It was a map of sorts, pointing to a hidden location—an old, abandoned villa on the outskirts of Sevilla. According to the code, something valuable was hidden there, something that Isabella had been willing to kill for.

"We need to go there," Mia said, her voice filled with resolve. "We need to find whatever it is and expose Isabella's crimes."

Ivan nodded, his expression serious. "We should be careful. If Isabella knows we're onto her, she could be dangerous."

They agreed to set out the next morning, prepared for whatever they might find. As Mia lay in bed that night, she felt a mixture of anticipation and trepidation. The journey was nearing its climax, and she knew that the answers they sought were within reach.

Sleep came fitfully, filled with dreams of swirling patterns, hidden messages, and the boundless possibilities of her art and her investigation. Mia knew that the next day would bring new challenges, but she was ready to face them with courage and determination.

The journey was just beginning, and she was ready to embrace it with open arms and an open heart.

Chapter 10: Danger Lurks

The morning light filtered through the hotel room curtains, casting a soft glow over the room. Mia sat up in bed, her mind still swirling with the events of the previous day. The hidden code in Luis's paintings had given them a crucial lead, but it also meant they were venturing into dangerous territory. She knew that confronting Isabella could have serious consequences.

After a quick breakfast, Mia met Ivan in the hotel lobby. He looked determined but cautious, a reflection of her own feelings. They had agreed to visit the abandoned villa mentioned in the code, hoping to find whatever treasure or information Isabella had been so desperate to keep hidden.

"Ready?" Ivan asked, his eyes meeting hers with a mix of resolve and concern.

Mia nodded. "Ready. Let's find out what Isabella has been hiding."

They set out for the villa, located on the outskirts of Sevilla. The drive was quiet, both of them lost in their thoughts. The countryside around them was beautiful, but there was an undercurrent of tension that neither could shake.

As they approached the villa, the landscape grew more desolate. The building itself was a grand, albeit decaying, structure that spoke of former glory. It was clear that no one had lived there for years. Mia and Ivan parked the car a short distance away and approached on foot, their eyes scanning the area for any signs of danger.

"Stay close," Ivan said, his voice low and tense. "We don't know what—or who—might be waiting for us."

Mia nodded, feeling a thrill of fear and excitement. They reached the entrance of the villa, the door hanging loosely on its hinges. With a deep breath, they stepped inside, their footsteps echoing in the empty hallways.

The interior was just as dilapidated as the exterior, with dust and debris covering the floor. They moved cautiously, their flashlights cutting through the darkness. It wasn't long before they found a room that seemed to match the description in the code—a library, with tall shelves filled with old, musty books.

"According to the code, whatever we're looking for should be hidden here," Mia said, her voice barely above a whisper.

They began to search the room, examining the shelves and the books. It was painstaking work, but they were driven by the knowledge that they were close to uncovering the truth. After what felt like hours, Ivan's flashlight caught something unusual—a small, hidden compartment behind one of the shelves.

"Mia, over here," Ivan called softly, prying the compartment open.

Inside, they found a small chest, locked and covered in dust. Mia's heart raced as they carefully removed it and set it on a nearby table. Ivan produced a small set of tools from his bag and began to work on the lock. After a few tense minutes, it clicked open.

They lifted the lid to reveal a collection of documents and a few pieces of jewelry. Mia carefully picked up the documents, her eyes scanning the pages. They were old letters and contracts, detailing a series of art deals and financial transactions that linked Isabella to a network of illegal activities, including money laundering and art theft.

"This is it," Mia said, her voice trembling with excitement and fear. "This is the proof we need to expose Isabella."

Ivan nodded, his eyes serious. "We need to get these to Inspector Ruiz as soon as possible. This could be dangerous if Isabella finds out we have them."

They carefully packed up the documents and jewelry, making sure everything was secure. As they prepared to leave, they heard a noise from outside—a car approaching. Mia's heart skipped a beat as they quickly hid behind one of the shelves, peeking out to see who was arriving.

A sleek, black car pulled up to the villa, and a tall, imposing figure stepped out. It was Isabella, her expression cold and calculating. She was accompanied by two men who looked like hired muscle, their eyes scanning the area for any signs of intruders.

"We need to get out of here, now," Ivan whispered, his voice urgent.

Mia nodded, her heart pounding. They carefully made their way to the back of the villa, avoiding the front entrance where Isabella and her men were. As they reached a side door, Mia's foot caught on a loose floorboard, causing a loud creak.

"Did you hear that?" one of the men said, his voice sharp.

Mia and Ivan froze, holding their breath. The men began to move toward the sound, their footsteps heavy on the wooden floor. Mia's mind raced, trying to come up with a plan. They couldn't afford to be caught now, not when they were so close to exposing Isabella's crimes.

"Follow me," Ivan whispered, leading Mia toward a narrow staircase that led to the basement.

They hurried down the stairs, the darkness closing in around them. The basement was even more decrepit than the rest of the villa, with crumbling walls and a damp, musty smell. They found a small window near the ceiling, just large enough to squeeze through.

"I'll go first and help you out," Ivan said, boosting himself up and through the window.

Mia followed, struggling to pull herself up and through the narrow opening. Ivan grabbed her hands and helped her the rest of the way, and they tumbled out into the overgrown garden behind the villa. They could hear the men searching the villa above them, their voices growing louder.

"We need to move, now," Ivan said, taking Mia's hand and leading her toward the tree line.

They ran through the dense underbrush, the sounds of their pursuers fading as they put distance between themselves and the villa.

After what felt like an eternity, they reached a small clearing and paused to catch their breath.

"That was close," Mia said, her voice shaking with adrenaline.

"Too close," Ivan replied, his eyes scanning the trees for any signs of movement. "We need to get back to the city and give these documents to Inspector Ruiz. Isabella won't stop until she gets them back."

They continued their trek through the forest, eventually reaching the road where they had parked the car. With one last cautious glance behind them, they got into the car and drove back to Sevilla, their minds racing with the implications of what they had found.

As they reached the city, they headed straight for the police station. Inspector Ruiz was waiting for them, his expression a mix of concern and curiosity.

"We found something," Mia said, handing him the documents. "These prove that Isabella was involved in illegal activities with Alejandro. She was using him to launder money and steal art."

Ruiz examined the documents, his eyes widening as he read through the evidence. "This is significant. We can use this to bring Isabella in for questioning and hopefully get to the bottom of Alejandro's death."

Mia and Ivan felt a wave of relief wash over them. They had finally uncovered the truth and had the proof they needed to bring justice for Alejandro. But they knew that the danger wasn't over yet.

"Be careful," Ruiz warned them. "Isabella is powerful and dangerous. She won't take this lightly."

"We will," Ivan replied, his expression resolute. "We'll do whatever it takes to see this through."

As they left the police station, Mia felt a sense of accomplishment and determination. They had come so far and faced so many challenges, but they were finally on the brink of exposing Isabella's crimes.

That night, as Mia lay in bed, she felt a mix of exhaustion and hope. The journey had been long and dangerous, but she knew they were making a difference. With Ivan by her side, she felt ready to face whatever challenges lay ahead.

Sleep came slowly, her dreams filled with swirling patterns, hidden messages, and the boundless possibilities of her art and her investigation. The journey was nearing its climax, and she was ready to embrace it with open arms and an open heart.

Chapter 11: A Brush with the Past

The next morning, Mia awoke with a renewed sense of determination. They had made significant progress, but the danger was far from over. Isabella's influence and reach were considerable, and Mia knew they had to be vigilant. She got ready quickly and met Ivan in the hotel lobby, his expression mirroring her own resolve.

"Good morning," Ivan greeted her, giving her a quick hug. "Ready to dive back into the investigation?"

"Absolutely," Mia replied, her voice steady. "We need to make sure Isabella is brought to justice and that we understand the full extent of her involvement."

They headed to the police station to follow up with Inspector Ruiz. The documents they had found at the villa were crucial, but there were still many unanswered questions. As they arrived, Ruiz was already busy, poring over the evidence they had provided.

"Good morning, Inspector," Mia said as they approached his desk. "Have you found anything new?"

Ruiz looked up, his expression serious. "Good morning. We've been examining the documents, and they confirm what you suspected. Isabella was deeply involved in illegal activities, using Alejandro to launder money and acquire stolen art. We're issuing a warrant for her arrest, but we need to move carefully. She has powerful connections."

Mia and Ivan exchanged a glance, understanding the gravity of the situation. "What can we do to help?" Ivan asked.

"Stay vigilant and keep investigating. There's a chance Isabella has hidden more evidence or has allies who could interfere," Ruiz replied. "We also need to understand more about the hidden message in those paintings. If Isabella was so desperate to acquire them, there must be a reason."

Mia nodded, feeling a sense of urgency. "We'll keep looking. There's one place I haven't checked thoroughly yet—Alejandro's old studio. He used to let me work there when I first started out, and it's possible he left something behind."

With Ruiz's encouragement, Mia and Ivan set off for Alejandro's old studio. The building was located in a quiet part of the city, away from the bustling tourist areas. It had been years since Mia had visited, and the memories of her early days as an artist flooded back as they approached.

The studio was a small, unassuming building, its exterior showing signs of neglect. They unlocked the door and stepped inside, the familiar scent of paint and turpentine greeting them. Dust motes danced in the sunlight streaming through the windows, and the space felt frozen in time.

Mia took a deep breath, feeling a wave of nostalgia. "I spent so many hours here, learning and creating. Alejandro was a great mentor."

Ivan squeezed her hand, offering silent support. "Let's see what we can find."

They began to search the studio, examining old canvases, sketchbooks, and boxes of art supplies. Mia felt a mixture of sadness and determination as she sifted through the remnants of her past. After a while, she found an old sketchbook that she didn't recognize. It was tucked away in a corner, covered in dust.

"Look at this," Mia said, holding up the sketchbook. "I don't remember seeing this before."

They opened the sketchbook and began to flip through the pages. It was filled with intricate sketches and notes, many of them detailing Alejandro's thoughts and ideas. As they reached the middle of the book, they found a series of sketches that caught their attention. They were rough drafts of the paintings Luis Ramirez had created—the ones that contained the hidden code.

"This must be it," Ivan said, his voice filled with excitement. "These sketches might hold the key to understanding the hidden message."

Mia carefully examined the sketches, her eyes scanning the details. She noticed that Alejandro had made notes in the margins, detailing his thoughts on the symbols and patterns. One note, in particular, stood out.

"This pattern corresponds to an ancient map," Mia read aloud. "It leads to a hidden location where a valuable artifact is buried."

Ivan's eyes widened. "That must be what Isabella was after. She believed the paintings would lead her to this artifact."

Mia nodded, her heart racing. "We need to find this map and see where it leads. If we can uncover the artifact, we might be able to use it as leverage against Isabella."

They continued to study the sketches, piecing together the fragments of the map. It was a complex puzzle, but Alejandro's notes provided crucial clues. After several hours of intense work, they finally had a clear picture of the map's location.

"It's an old monastery on the outskirts of the city," Mia said, pointing to a spot on the map. "That's where we need to go."

Ivan nodded, his expression serious. "We should be careful. If Isabella realizes we're close to finding the artifact, she might try to stop us."

With a plan in place, they set out for the monastery. The drive was tense, both of them on high alert for any signs of danger. The monastery was a secluded and ancient building, its stone walls weathered by centuries of history. They parked the car a short distance away and approached on foot, their eyes scanning the area for any signs of Isabella or her associates.

The monastery was eerily quiet as they stepped inside, the only sound the soft echo of their footsteps. They followed the map's directions, winding through the labyrinthine corridors and down into the depths of the building. The air grew colder as they descended, the light dimming until they were forced to rely on their flashlights.

Mia's heart pounded in her chest as they reached a hidden chamber, the door marked with symbols matching those in the paintings. "This is it," she whispered, her voice trembling with anticipation.

They pushed open the door and stepped inside. The chamber was small and dark, with a single stone pedestal in the center. On the pedestal rested a small, ornate box, its surface covered in intricate carvings.

Mia approached the box cautiously, her hands shaking as she lifted the lid. Inside, she found a collection of ancient scrolls and a small, golden artifact—a beautifully crafted amulet that seemed to glow with an inner light.

"This must be the artifact," Mia said, her voice filled with awe. "It's incredible."

Ivan examined the scrolls, his expression serious. "These documents are ancient. They could be worth a fortune."

As they carefully packed up the artifact and scrolls, Mia felt a surge of triumph. They had found the treasure Isabella had been so desperate to obtain. But she knew their journey was far from over. They needed to get these items to Inspector Ruiz and ensure that Isabella was brought to justice.

As they made their way back to the surface, Mia and Ivan remained vigilant. They knew that Isabella wouldn't give up easily, and they needed to stay one step ahead. The drive back to the city was tense, both of them on high alert for any signs of danger.

When they arrived at the police station, Inspector Ruiz was waiting for them. His eyes widened as they showed him the artifact and the scrolls, understanding the significance of their find.

"This is incredible," Ruiz said, his voice filled with awe. "With this evidence, we can finally bring Isabella to justice."

Mia and Ivan felt a wave of relief wash over them. They had uncovered the truth and found the proof they needed. But they knew that the danger wasn't over yet.

"We need to move quickly," Ruiz said, his expression serious. "Isabella won't give up without a fight."

That night, as Mia lay in bed, she felt a mix of exhaustion and hope. The journey had been long and dangerous, but they were finally on the brink of bringing justice for Alejandro. With Ivan by her side and the support of Inspector Ruiz, she felt ready to face whatever challenges lay ahead.

Sleep came slowly, her dreams filled with swirling patterns, hidden messages, and the boundless possibilities of her art and her investigation. The journey was nearing its climax, and she was ready to embrace it with open arms and an open heart.

Chapter 12: The Artist's Confession

The first light of dawn filtered through the curtains, casting a soft glow over Mia's room. She woke with a sense of purpose, the events of the previous day still fresh in her mind. They were closer than ever to bringing Isabella to justice, but the danger was far from over. After a quick breakfast, she met Ivan in the hotel lobby, both of them ready to continue their investigation.

"Good morning, Mia," Ivan greeted her with a quick hug. "How did you sleep?"

"Not much, but I'm ready to keep going," Mia replied, her eyes filled with determination. "We need to speak with Luis Ramirez again. He might have more information about the hidden messages in the paintings."

Ivan nodded. "I agree. Let's head to his studio and see what else he can tell us."

They set off for Luis's studio, their minds racing with thoughts of the hidden artifact and Isabella's involvement. The streets of Sevilla were just beginning to come to life, the city awakening with the promise of a new day. When they arrived at the studio, Luis was already there, working on a new piece of art.

"Luis, we need to talk," Mia said as they entered, her tone urgent but respectful.

Luis looked up, his expression curious but wary. "What is it? Did you find something?"

Mia and Ivan explained their discovery at the monastery and the significance of the hidden messages in the paintings. Luis listened intently, his face growing more serious with each new piece of information.

"I knew there was something special about those paintings," Luis said, his voice filled with awe. "But I had no idea they contained such a valuable secret."

"Do you remember anything else about the creation of those paintings?" Ivan asked. "Anything that might help us understand why Isabella was so desperate to obtain them?"

Luis hesitated, his eyes flickering with uncertainty. "There was something... Alejandro was very particular about the symbols and patterns. He said they were part of an ancient code, something that had been passed down through generations. He mentioned a book that he had used as a reference, an old manuscript that he kept hidden."

Mia's heart skipped a beat. "Do you know where we can find this book?"

Luis thought for a moment, then nodded. "Alejandro kept it in a safe place. He told me once that if anything ever happened to him, I should look for it in his personal study at his home. It's hidden behind a false panel in the bookshelf."

"Thank you, Luis," Mia said, her voice filled with gratitude. "You've been a great help."

As they left the studio, Mia and Ivan felt a renewed sense of urgency. They needed to find the manuscript and uncover any additional information it might contain. The journey to Alejandro's home was filled with anticipation, both of them eager to find the next piece of the puzzle.

When they arrived, they were greeted by Alejandro's housekeeper, who had been maintaining the property since his death. She allowed them inside, understanding the importance of their search. Mia led the way to Alejandro's personal study, a room filled with books, artifacts, and memories.

"Let's start looking for that false panel," Ivan suggested, moving toward the bookshelf.

They carefully examined the shelves, feeling for any signs of a hidden compartment. After a few minutes, Mia's fingers brushed against a small latch hidden behind a row of books. She pressed it, and a section of the bookshelf swung open, revealing a small, hidden alcove.

Inside the alcove was an old, leather-bound manuscript. Mia gently removed it, her hands trembling with excitement. The cover was worn and faded, the pages yellowed with age. She carefully opened the book, revealing intricate illustrations and handwritten notes.

"This must be it," Mia whispered, her eyes scanning the pages. "This is the key to understanding the code in the paintings."

Ivan leaned over her shoulder, his eyes wide with awe. "We need to study this carefully. It might contain information that can help us bring Isabella to justice."

They spent the next few hours pouring over the manuscript, deciphering the symbols and notes. It was a painstaking process, but gradually, a clearer picture began to emerge. The manuscript detailed the history of the artifact they had found, describing its significance and the power it held. It also included a detailed account of the code in the paintings, explaining how it could be used to locate the artifact and unlock its secrets.

"This is incredible," Mia said, her voice filled with awe. "Alejandro must have known the importance of this artifact and the danger it posed in the wrong hands."

"We need to take this to Inspector Ruiz," Ivan said, his tone serious. "This manuscript, along with the artifact and the documents we found, should be enough to bring Isabella to justice."

As they prepared to leave, Mia felt a deep sense of gratitude for Alejandro. He had protected this valuable information, ensuring that it would be found by those who could use it for good. She knew that their journey was far from over, but they were one step closer to achieving their goal.

Back at the police station, Inspector Ruiz listened intently as Mia and Ivan presented their findings. His eyes widened as he examined the manuscript, understanding the significance of what they had discovered.

"This is extraordinary," Ruiz said, his voice filled with admiration. "With this evidence, we can finally bring Isabella to justice. But we need to be careful. She's dangerous and won't go down without a fight."

Mia and Ivan nodded, understanding the gravity of the situation. They had come too far to back down now, and they were determined to see this through to the end.

As they left the police station, Mia felt a mixture of exhaustion and hope. They had uncovered crucial information, but the danger was far from over. She knew that they needed to stay vigilant and continue their investigation, but with Ivan by her side and the support of Inspector Ruiz, she felt ready to face whatever challenges lay ahead.

That evening, as they sat in a quiet café, Mia and Ivan discussed their next steps. They knew that they needed to find a way to bring Isabella in without alerting her to their plans.

"We should set a trap," Ivan suggested, his eyes filled with determination. "If we can lure her out into the open, we can catch her off guard and ensure she's brought to justice."

Mia nodded, her mind racing with possibilities. "We need to be smart about this. We can't let her slip through our fingers."

They spent the next few hours devising a plan, carefully considering every detail. They knew that their window of opportunity was small, and they needed to act quickly and decisively.

As they left the café, Mia felt a renewed sense of purpose. The journey had been long and dangerous, but they were finally on the brink of bringing justice for Alejandro. With Ivan by her side and the support of Inspector Ruiz, she felt ready to face whatever challenges lay ahead.

That night, as Mia lay in bed, she felt a mix of exhaustion and hope. The journey had been long and dangerous, but they were finally on the brink of bringing justice for Alejandro. With Ivan by her side, she felt ready to face whatever challenges lay ahead.

Sleep came slowly, her dreams filled with swirling patterns, hidden messages, and the boundless possibilities of her art and her investigation. The journey was nearing its climax, and she was ready to embrace it with open arms and an open heart.

Chapter 13: Hidden in Plain Sight

The dawn broke gently over Sevilla, casting the city in a warm, golden light. Mia awoke feeling both the weight of their discoveries and the urgency of their mission. Today was the day they would set their trap for Isabella, and the stakes had never been higher.

After a quick breakfast, she met Ivan in the hotel lobby. His expression was a mirror of her own—determined, focused, and slightly anxious. They knew what they had to do, but the risks were significant.

"Morning, Mia. Ready for this?" Ivan asked, giving her a reassuring smile.

"Ready as I'll ever be," Mia replied, taking a deep breath. "Let's make sure we have everything in place."

Their first stop was the police station to finalize their plans with Inspector Ruiz. The inspector greeted them with a nod, his expression serious. "Good morning. We've reviewed your plan, and it looks solid. We'll have officers in place to assist and ensure everything goes smoothly."

Mia and Ivan laid out their strategy. They would lure Isabella to a public place under the pretense of negotiating the return of the artifact and the documents. It was risky, but they hoped that the promise of reclaiming her precious items would be too tempting for Isabella to resist.

"We need to choose a location where we can control the environment," Ivan said, his voice steady. "How about the Plaza de España? It's open, but we can position officers around to ensure she doesn't have a chance to escape."

Ruiz nodded. "Good choice. It's a public space, so she'll feel secure, but we can easily cover all the exits. Let's set it for this afternoon."

With the plan in place, Mia and Ivan left the police station to prepare for the meeting. They felt a mix of anxiety and anticipation, knowing that they were close to bringing Isabella to justice.

As the afternoon approached, they made their way to the Plaza de España. The beautiful, semi-circular plaza was one of Sevilla's most iconic landmarks, its majestic architecture providing a stunning backdrop for their confrontation. Mia and Ivan took their positions, scanning the area for any signs of Isabella or her associates.

Inspector Ruiz and his team were discreetly positioned around the plaza, ready to act at a moment's notice. Mia felt a surge of nervous energy as the time for the meeting approached. She knew they had to stay focused and alert.

"Here she comes," Ivan whispered, nodding towards a sleek, black car that had just pulled up. Isabella stepped out, her expression confident and calculating. She was accompanied by two men, who flanked her protectively.

Mia took a deep breath and stepped forward, holding the small, ornate box containing the artifact. "Isabella, thank you for coming."

Isabella's eyes narrowed as she approached, her gaze flicking between Mia and Ivan. "I want my artifact and the documents. Hand them over, and this will all be over."

"Not so fast," Mia said, her voice steady. "We need to talk first. There are conditions."

Isabella's expression hardened. "Conditions? You're in no position to make demands."

Ivan stepped forward, his tone firm. "Actually, we are. We have enough evidence to expose your illegal activities and bring you to justice. But we're willing to negotiate. If you cooperate, we can make things easier for you."

For a moment, Isabella seemed to consider their offer. But then, her eyes flashed with anger. "I don't think so. I want the artifact, now."

As she spoke, her two bodyguards moved forward, their intentions clear. Mia's heart pounded in her chest, but she stood her ground. Just as the tension reached its peak, Inspector Ruiz and his officers stepped out from their hiding places, surrounding Isabella and her men.

"Isabella Martinez, you're under arrest," Ruiz announced, his voice commanding. "Surrender now, and no one will get hurt."

Isabella's eyes widened in shock and fury. For a moment, it seemed like she might try to resist, but then she raised her hands in defeat. Her bodyguards, seeing the overwhelming force around them, followed suit.

As the officers moved in to take Isabella and her men into custody, Mia felt a wave of relief wash over her. They had done it. They had finally brought Isabella to justice.

Inspector Ruiz approached Mia and Ivan, a satisfied smile on his face. "Excellent work. Thanks to your efforts, we've been able to put an end to Isabella's operations and bring closure to Alejandro's death."

"Thank you, Inspector," Mia said, her voice filled with gratitude. "We couldn't have done it without your help."

Ruiz nodded. "This is a victory for all of us. Now, let's make sure Isabella faces the full extent of the law."

As the police escorted Isabella and her associates away, Mia and Ivan took a moment to reflect on their journey. They had faced numerous challenges and dangers, but they had persevered. Their determination and teamwork had brought them to this moment of triumph.

Later that evening, Mia and Ivan found themselves at a quiet café, the tension of the day slowly melting away. They sat together, their hands intertwined, savoring the moment of peace and accomplishment.

"We did it, Mia," Ivan said, his voice filled with pride. "We really did it."

Mia smiled, her eyes sparkling with relief and happiness. "Yes, we did. And I couldn't have done it without you, Ivan."

They toasted to their success, the clinking of their glasses a symbol of their hard-fought victory. As they sat together, enjoying the warmth of the evening and the satisfaction of a job well done, Mia felt a deep sense of gratitude for the journey they had shared.

That night, as Mia lay in bed, she felt a mix of exhaustion and contentment. The journey had been long and dangerous, but they had finally brought justice for Alejandro. With Ivan by her side and the support of Inspector Ruiz, she felt ready to face whatever challenges lay ahead.

Sleep came slowly, her dreams filled with swirling patterns, hidden messages, and the boundless possibilities of her art and her future. The journey had reached its climax, and she was ready to embrace the next chapter with open arms and an open heart.

Chapter 14: The Photographer's Insight

The sun rose over Sevilla, casting a golden glow on the city's historic buildings. Mia awoke with a sense of accomplishment and a lingering exhaustion from the events of the previous day. They had succeeded in bringing Isabella to justice, but the mystery of the hidden messages in the paintings still tugged at her mind. There was more to uncover, and she felt a renewed sense of purpose.

After breakfast, Mia met Ivan at the gallery. He greeted her with a warm smile and a quick hug. "Good morning, Mia. How are you feeling?"

"Relieved, but still curious," Mia replied. "We need to understand more about the messages in the paintings. There's still so much we don't know."

Ivan nodded, his expression thoughtful. "I've been thinking about that too. I believe my photography skills could help us analyze the paintings further. We might be able to uncover details that aren't visible to the naked eye."

Intrigued, Mia agreed. They decided to bring Luis Ramirez back into the fold, knowing his insights could be invaluable. They contacted him and arranged to meet at his studio later that morning.

Luis welcomed them with a curious smile, his eyes bright with anticipation. "Mia, Ivan, good to see you both. What brings you back?"

"We need your help, Luis," Mia explained. "We believe there are still hidden messages in the paintings, and Ivan thinks his photography skills can help us uncover them."

Luis's eyes widened with interest. "I'd be happy to help. Let's get started."

They set up the paintings in Luis's studio, adjusting the lighting to create the best conditions for Ivan's photography. Ivan unpacked his camera and various lenses, explaining his plan to Mia and Luis.

"We'll use different types of light—infrared, ultraviolet, and polarized light—to reveal any hidden layers or details in the paintings," Ivan said, his voice filled with excitement. "It's a technique used in art restoration and forensics, and it can uncover things that are invisible to the naked eye."

As Ivan began to take photographs, Mia and Luis watched with anticipation. The process was meticulous, each shot requiring careful adjustment and precision. Mia felt a growing sense of excitement, knowing they were on the brink of uncovering more secrets.

Hours passed as Ivan worked, the studio filled with the soft click of the camera and the hum of conversation. Finally, Ivan stepped back, a satisfied smile on his face. "I think we've got it. Let's take a look."

They gathered around Ivan's laptop as he transferred the images. The first set of photographs revealed subtle variations in the paint, hinting at hidden layers beneath. As Ivan adjusted the settings, more details began to emerge—faint lines, symbols, and patterns that had been concealed for centuries.

"This is incredible," Luis said, his voice filled with awe. "I had no idea there was so much hidden in these paintings."

Mia felt a surge of excitement as she examined the images. The symbols and patterns seemed to form a complex code, one that she was determined to decipher. "We need to analyze these carefully. There's a pattern here, something that connects all the paintings."

They spent the rest of the day examining the photographs, comparing notes, and discussing their findings. It was a painstaking process, but gradually, a clearer picture began to emerge. The hidden messages seemed to tell a story, one that spanned generations and connected to an ancient secret.

As they worked, Mia felt a deepening connection with Ivan. Their shared passion for uncovering the truth brought them closer together, and she was grateful for his support and expertise. By the time they finished, the sun had set, and the studio was bathed in the warm glow of the evening light.

"We've made a lot of progress," Mia said, her voice filled with satisfaction. "But there's still more to uncover. We need to continue our research and see where this leads."

Luis nodded, his expression thoughtful. "I agree. These paintings hold a treasure trove of secrets, and we're only just beginning to understand them."

As they packed up for the day, Ivan suggested they take a break and enjoy the evening. "We've been working hard. Let's go for a walk and clear our minds. It might help us see things more clearly."

Mia agreed, feeling the need to relax and recharge. They said goodbye to Luis and left the studio, stepping out into the cool evening air. The streets of Sevilla were alive with activity, the vibrant energy of the city a welcome contrast to the intensity of their investigation.

As they walked, Ivan took Mia's hand, their fingers intertwining. "I'm really proud of what we've accomplished, Mia. We've come so far, and I know we'll uncover the rest of the mystery."

Mia smiled, her heart filled with warmth. "I couldn't have done it without you, Ivan. Your skills and support have been invaluable."

They wandered through the narrow streets, the sounds of laughter and music filling the air. The city's charm was undeniable, and Mia felt a sense of peace as they explored together. They eventually found a quiet café and settled into a cozy corner, enjoying the ambiance and each other's company.

"I've been thinking," Ivan said, his voice thoughtful. "Once we've finished this investigation, we should consider working on a project together. Your art and my photography—it could be something really special."

Mia's eyes lit up with excitement. "I'd love that, Ivan. I think our styles complement each other, and it would be amazing to create something together."

They spent the rest of the evening discussing ideas, their conversation filled with enthusiasm and inspiration. The bond between them grew stronger with each passing moment, and Mia felt a deep sense of contentment.

As they walked back to their hotel, Mia felt a renewed sense of purpose. They had made significant progress, but the journey was far from over. With Ivan by her side, she felt ready to face whatever challenges lay ahead.

That night, as Mia lay in bed, her mind raced with thoughts of their discoveries and the possibilities for the future. She knew they were on the brink of something extraordinary, and she was eager to continue their journey.

Sleep came slowly, her dreams filled with swirling patterns, hidden messages, and the boundless possibilities of her art and her collaboration with Ivan. The journey was unfolding beautifully, and she was ready to embrace it with open arms and an open heart.

Chapter 15: Close Encounters

The morning sun filtered through the curtains, casting a warm glow over Mia's room. She awoke with a sense of anticipation, knowing that their investigation was far from over. After a quick breakfast, she met Ivan in the hotel lobby, both of them eager to continue their work on the hidden messages in the paintings.

"Morning, Mia. Ready to dive back in?" Ivan greeted her with a quick hug.

"Absolutely. Let's see what more we can uncover," Mia replied, her eyes bright with determination.

They headed back to Luis's studio, where the paintings and the photographs from the previous day awaited them. Luis greeted them with a warm smile, his excitement palpable. "Good morning! I've been thinking about our findings and I have some new ideas."

They gathered around the table where the photographs were laid out, studying the intricate details that Ivan's camera had captured. The hidden symbols and patterns seemed to form a complex narrative, one that was slowly coming into focus.

"We need to decipher these symbols," Mia said, her voice filled with resolve. "They hold the key to understanding the full story."

Luis nodded. "I agree. I've been researching ancient codes and symbols, and I think I've found some references that could help us."

They spent the morning cross-referencing the symbols in the photographs with ancient texts and manuscripts that Luis had unearthed. It was meticulous work, but gradually, a clearer picture began to emerge. The symbols appeared to tell the story of an ancient artifact, one that had been hidden away to protect it from those who sought its power.

"This is incredible," Luis said, his voice filled with awe. "These paintings are like a treasure map, leading to something of great historical significance."

Mia felt a thrill of excitement. "We're getting closer. But we need to be careful. If Isabella was willing to go to such lengths to obtain the artifact, there may be others who are just as dangerous."

As they worked, Mia couldn't shake the feeling that they were being watched. She glanced around the studio, but saw nothing out of the ordinary. The sense of unease lingered, but she pushed it aside, focusing on the task at hand.

By late afternoon, they had made significant progress in deciphering the symbols. The paintings seemed to point to a specific location—an old, abandoned monastery in the hills outside Sevilla. According to the texts they had referenced, the monastery had once been a place of great importance, a sanctuary where the artifact had been hidden for safekeeping.

"We need to go there," Ivan said, his voice filled with determination. "If the artifact is still there, we need to find it before anyone else does."

Mia agreed, feeling a mix of excitement and apprehension. "Let's gather our things and head out. The sooner we get there, the better."

They packed up their notes and equipment, ready to set off for the monastery. As they left the studio, Mia couldn't shake the feeling that they were being followed. She glanced over her shoulder, but saw no one. The streets of Sevilla were bustling with activity, but she couldn't pinpoint the source of her unease.

"Something's not right," Mia whispered to Ivan as they walked. "I feel like we're being watched."

Ivan's expression grew serious. "Stay close. We'll keep an eye out."

They reached their car and set off for the monastery, the tension in the air palpable. The drive through the hills was beautiful, the landscape bathed in the golden light of the setting sun. But Mia's mind was focused on the task ahead and the sense of danger that seemed to follow them.

As they approached the monastery, the road grew narrower and more secluded. The ancient building loomed ahead, its stone walls weathered by time. They parked the car and approached cautiously, their eyes scanning the surroundings for any signs of movement.

The monastery was eerily quiet, the only sound the rustle of leaves in the breeze. They made their way inside, the interior dark and filled with the musty scent of age. Mia felt a chill run down her spine as they explored the labyrinthine corridors, their footsteps echoing in the silence.

"This place is incredible," Luis whispered, his voice filled with awe. "It's like stepping back in time."

They followed the clues from the paintings, which led them deeper into the monastery. The symbols guided them to a hidden chamber, its entrance concealed behind a large tapestry. Mia's heart raced as they pushed the tapestry aside and stepped inside.

The chamber was small and dimly lit, with a single stone pedestal in the center. On the pedestal rested a small, ornate box, its surface covered in intricate carvings. Mia felt a surge of excitement and trepidation as she approached the box, her hands trembling with anticipation.

"This must be it," she whispered, carefully lifting the lid.

Inside, they found a collection of ancient scrolls and a small, golden amulet—an artifact that seemed to glow with an inner light. Mia felt a sense of awe as she held the amulet, its significance clear.

"This is the artifact," Luis said, his voice filled with wonder. "It's been hidden here for centuries."

As they examined the scrolls, they realized they had uncovered something of great historical importance. The scrolls detailed the history of the artifact, its power, and the lengths to which people had gone to protect it.

"This is incredible," Ivan said, his eyes wide with amazement. "We need to get this to Inspector Ruiz. This could change everything."

As they prepared to leave, Mia's sense of unease returned. She glanced around the chamber, her eyes scanning the shadows. Suddenly, a figure stepped out of the darkness, blocking their exit.

"Well, well, what do we have here?" the man said, his voice cold and menacing.

Mia's heart pounded in her chest as she recognized him—it was one of Isabella's associates, a man she had seen with her during the confrontation at the plaza. He was flanked by two other men, their expressions hard and threatening.

"You've found the artifact," the man continued, his eyes glinting with malice. "Hand it over, and no one gets hurt."

Mia felt a surge of fear, but she stood her ground. "We're not giving you anything. This artifact belongs to the world, not to those who would misuse it."

The man's expression darkened. "I'm afraid you don't have a choice."

Before Mia could react, the men lunged at them. Ivan stepped forward, his fists raised in defense. A struggle ensued, the confined space of the chamber making it difficult to move. Mia clutched the artifact to her chest, her heart racing.

Luis, though not a fighter, grabbed a nearby object and swung it at one of the men, buying Ivan a moment to gain the upper hand. With a swift movement, Ivan knocked one of the attackers to the ground, but the other two were still advancing.

"We need to get out of here!" Mia shouted, her voice filled with urgency.

Using their combined strength, they managed to push past the attackers and make a break for the exit. The dark corridors of the monastery seemed to stretch endlessly, but they kept running, fueled by adrenaline and fear.

As they burst out into the open air, Mia felt a sense of relief, but she knew they weren't safe yet. They sprinted to the car, Ivan quickly starting the engine and speeding away from the monastery. Mia glanced back, her heart still pounding.

"We did it," she said, her voice trembling with relief. "But we need to get this to Inspector Ruiz immediately."

They drove back to Sevilla, the tension in the car palpable. When they arrived at the police station, they were greeted by a surprised but relieved Inspector Ruiz.

"Mia, Ivan, what happened?" he asked, his eyes wide with concern.

"We found the artifact," Mia said, holding up the small, golden amulet. "But we were ambushed by Isabella's associates. We need to make sure this is kept safe."

Ruiz's expression hardened. "You did well. We'll ensure the artifact is protected and that those responsible are brought to justice."

As they handed over the artifact and the scrolls, Mia felt a sense of accomplishment and relief. They had faced great danger, but they had succeeded in their mission. The artifact was safe, and Isabella's network was being dismantled.

That night, as Mia lay in bed, she felt a mix of exhaustion and contentment. The journey had been long and perilous, but they had uncovered the truth and brought justice for Alejandro. With Ivan by her side, she felt ready to face whatever challenges lay ahead.

Sleep came slowly, her dreams filled with swirling patterns, hidden messages, and the boundless possibilities of her art and her future. The journey had reached a critical point, and she was ready to embrace the next chapter with open arms and an open heart.

Chapter 16: The Breakthrough

The morning sun streamed through the curtains, casting a warm glow over Mia's room. She stretched and felt a sense of accomplishment mixed with a lingering exhaustion from the previous day's events. They had faced danger and succeeded in protecting the artifact, but she knew their work was far from over. After a quick breakfast, she met Ivan in the hotel lobby. His expression mirrored her own determination.

"Morning, Mia. Ready to keep going?" Ivan asked, giving her a reassuring smile.

"Absolutely. We've come this far, and I'm not stopping now," Mia replied, her eyes filled with resolve.

Their first stop was the police station, where they were scheduled to meet with Inspector Ruiz. They needed to follow up on the investigation and see what progress had been made with the artifact and the scrolls. Ruiz greeted them with a nod, his expression serious but encouraging.

"Good morning. I have some updates for you," Ruiz said, motioning for them to sit down. "Our experts have examined the artifact and the scrolls. They confirm that the scrolls contain valuable historical information and that the artifact is indeed significant. We're coordinating with historical and cultural institutions to ensure these items are preserved and studied properly."

Mia felt a surge of relief. "That's great news. What about Isabella's associates? Have they been apprehended?"

Ruiz nodded. "We've made several arrests based on the information you provided. Isabella's network is being dismantled, and we're confident we'll bring her remaining associates to justice. Your efforts have been instrumental in this investigation."

Mia and Ivan exchanged a glance, feeling a sense of accomplishment. But Mia couldn't shake the feeling that there was more to uncover. The hidden messages in the paintings had led them to the artifact, but she sensed there was still a deeper story waiting to be revealed.

"Inspector, we believe there might be more to this than just the artifact. The hidden messages in the paintings seemed to tell a larger story, one that might be connected to a broader historical context. We'd like to continue our research and see where it leads," Mia said, her voice steady.

Ruiz nodded thoughtfully. "I understand. Your dedication is admirable. Keep me informed of any new discoveries. We'll continue to support your efforts."

With renewed determination, Mia and Ivan left the police station and headed back to Luis's studio. They knew they needed to delve deeper into the hidden messages in the paintings and uncover the full story.

Luis greeted them with enthusiasm. "Good to see you both. I've been thinking about our findings, and I have some new ideas. The symbols in the paintings might be connected to a specific historical event or legend. We need to look at the broader context."

They spent the morning cross-referencing the symbols in the paintings with historical texts and manuscripts. Luis had unearthed several books and documents that could provide valuable insights. As they worked, Mia felt a growing sense of anticipation. They were on the brink of a breakthrough.

By late afternoon, they had made significant progress. The symbols and patterns in the paintings seemed to align with an ancient legend about a hidden treasure and a secret society dedicated to protecting it. The story spoke of a powerful artifact, one that had been hidden away to prevent it from falling into the wrong hands.

"This is incredible," Luis said, his voice filled with awe. "These paintings are like a map, guiding us to a hidden truth. The legend speaks of a treasure that could change the course of history."

Mia felt a thrill of excitement. "We're getting closer. We need to follow the clues and see where they lead. If we can uncover the full story, it could have profound implications."

As they continued their research, Ivan's photography skills once again proved invaluable. He used different lighting techniques to reveal hidden details in the paintings, uncovering symbols and patterns that had previously gone unnoticed. The paintings seemed to tell a story of a journey, one that led to a hidden location where the treasure was said to be buried.

"We need to find this location," Ivan said, his voice filled with determination. "If the legend is true, the treasure could be of immense historical value."

Mia nodded, feeling a sense of purpose. "Let's keep working. We're on the right track."

They spent the rest of the day piecing together the clues, their excitement growing with each new discovery. By evening, they had a clearer picture of the journey depicted in the paintings. The clues pointed to a remote location in the mountains outside Sevilla, a place that had been largely forgotten over time.

"This is it," Luis said, his eyes shining with excitement. "We need to go there and see what we can find."

Mia and Ivan agreed, feeling a sense of anticipation. They packed their equipment and set out early the next morning, determined to uncover the hidden treasure and the full story behind the paintings.

The drive through the mountains was breathtaking, the rugged landscape bathed in the soft light of dawn. Mia felt a sense of awe as they approached the location marked in the paintings. It was a remote and secluded area, far from the bustling city of Sevilla.

As they arrived at the site, Mia felt a surge of excitement. The area was overgrown with vegetation, and the ruins of an old structure were barely visible through the dense foliage. They carefully made their way through the underbrush, guided by the symbols in the paintings.

"This place is incredible," Ivan said, his voice filled with wonder. "It's like stepping into another world."

They reached a clearing where the remains of an ancient building stood. The walls were covered in moss and vines, but the structure was still intact. Mia felt a sense of reverence as they explored the ruins, their footsteps echoing in the silence.

"This must be the place," Luis said, examining the symbols etched into the stone walls. "The paintings led us here. There must be something hidden within these ruins."

They carefully searched the area, looking for any signs of the hidden treasure. It was a meticulous process, but their determination kept them going. Finally, Mia's hand brushed against a loose stone in the wall. She pushed it aside, revealing a hidden compartment.

"Look at this," she said, her voice filled with excitement.

Inside the compartment, they found a small chest, covered in dust and cobwebs. Mia carefully opened it, revealing a collection of ancient artifacts and scrolls. The items were beautifully preserved, their significance clear.

"This is it," Luis said, his voice trembling with awe. "We've found the hidden treasure."

Mia felt a surge of triumph. They had uncovered the full story behind the paintings and the legend. The artifacts and scrolls held immense historical value, providing a glimpse into a forgotten past.

"We need to get these to Inspector Ruiz," Ivan said, his voice filled with determination. "This is a major breakthrough."

They carefully packed the artifacts and made their way back to the car, their hearts filled with excitement and satisfaction. The drive back to Sevilla was filled with a sense of accomplishment and anticipation.

When they arrived at the police station, Inspector Ruiz was waiting for them. His eyes widened as they presented the artifacts and scrolls, understanding the significance of their discovery.

"This is extraordinary," Ruiz said, his voice filled with admiration. "You've uncovered a piece of history. These items will be preserved and studied, and their story will be shared with the world."

Mia and Ivan felt a wave of relief and satisfaction. They had completed their mission, uncovering the full story behind the paintings and the hidden treasure. With the support of Inspector Ruiz and the historical community, they knew that their discoveries would have a lasting impact.

That night, as Mia lay in bed, she felt a mix of exhaustion and contentment. The journey had been long and challenging, but they had succeeded in their mission. With Ivan by her side, she felt ready to face whatever challenges lay ahead.

Sleep came slowly, her dreams filled with swirling patterns, hidden messages, and the boundless possibilities of her art and her future. The journey had reached a new chapter, and she was ready to embrace it with open arms and an open heart.

Chapter 17: The Art Auction

The next morning, Mia woke with a renewed sense of purpose. The artifacts they had uncovered were safe with Inspector Ruiz, but she knew that the intrigue surrounding Isabella's network was far from over. There was still more to uncover, and Mia felt a deep resolve to see their mission through to the end.

After a quick breakfast, Mia met Ivan in the hotel lobby. His expression was a blend of determination and excitement. They were planning to attend a high-stakes art auction that evening, hoping to observe the suspects and gather more information about Isabella's network.

"Morning, Mia. Ready for tonight?" Ivan asked, giving her a reassuring smile.

"Absolutely. This auction could be our chance to learn more about Isabella's associates and their dealings," Mia replied, her eyes filled with resolve.

They spent the morning and afternoon preparing for the auction, researching the items on sale and the potential attendees. The auction was known for attracting high-profile collectors and influential figures in the art world, making it the perfect setting for their investigation.

As evening approached, Mia and Ivan dressed in their finest attire. Mia chose an elegant black dress that complemented her artistic flair, while Ivan donned a sharp suit. They needed to blend in with the sophisticated crowd to avoid drawing attention to themselves.

The auction was held at a grand estate on the outskirts of Sevilla, its opulent interior a testament to wealth and luxury. As they arrived, Mia felt a mix of excitement and apprehension. They were stepping into the lion's den, and they needed to be cautious.

"Stay close, and keep an eye on the key players," Ivan whispered as they entered the lavish ballroom where the auction was being held.

Mia nodded, her eyes scanning the room. The atmosphere was charged with anticipation, the crowd buzzing with conversations about the artworks on display. They mingled with the guests, engaging in polite small talk while discreetly observing the interactions around them.

It wasn't long before they spotted familiar faces—collectors and associates they had encountered during their investigation. Mia noticed Isabella's associate, the man who had ambushed them at the monastery, talking with a group of well-dressed individuals. She felt a surge of anger but kept her composure.

"We need to find out what they're up to," Mia whispered to Ivan, nodding towards the group.

Ivan nodded. "Let's split up and gather as much information as we can. Be careful."

Mia moved through the crowd, engaging in conversations and listening for any useful tidbits of information. She learned that several of the artworks on auction had dubious provenance, hinting at the illicit activities Isabella's network had been involved in.

As the auction began, Mia and Ivan took their seats, their eyes and ears attuned to the proceedings. The auctioneer introduced each piece with flourish, the bids escalating quickly as collectors vied for the prized artworks.

Mia noticed a particularly intense bidding war over a series of paintings that matched the style and symbolism of Luis Ramirez's work. The paintings were being sold by an anonymous seller, and the fierce competition suggested that they held more than just artistic value.

"Those paintings must be connected to Isabella's network," Mia whispered to Ivan. "We need to find out who's behind the sale."

Ivan nodded, his eyes focused on the bidders. "I'll see if I can get any information from the auction staff."

As the bidding continued, Mia felt a growing sense of urgency. The paintings were sold for an exorbitant amount, and she watched as the winning bidder, a wealthy collector named Rafael, signed the paperwork with a smug smile.

Mia decided to approach Rafael, hoping to learn more about his interest in the paintings. She waited until he was alone, then walked over with a confident smile.

"Congratulations on your purchase," Mia said, extending her hand. "I'm Mia Valdés, an artist and admirer of your collection."

Rafael shook her hand, his eyes gleaming with pride. "Thank you, Mia. I'm Rafael. These paintings are a remarkable addition to my collection."

"They certainly are. I couldn't help but notice the intense bidding. What drew you to these particular pieces?" Mia asked, her tone casual but inquisitive.

Rafael chuckled. "Ah, a fellow art enthusiast. There's something about the symbolism and history behind these paintings that fascinates me. They're said to contain hidden messages, a legacy of an ancient secret society."

Mia's heart raced. Rafael's interest in the paintings mirrored their own investigation. "That sounds intriguing. I've been researching similar themes in my work. Perhaps we could discuss it further?"

Rafael's eyes sparkled with interest. "I'd like that. How about a drink after the auction?"

Mia agreed, sensing an opportunity to gain valuable insights. As the auction concluded, she and Ivan regrouped, exchanging information about their findings. Ivan had learned that the anonymous seller was connected to a shell company, likely a front for Isabella's network.

"We need to stay close to Rafael. He might have more information than he realizes," Ivan said, his expression serious.

Mia nodded. "I've arranged to meet him for a drink. Let's see what we can uncover."

They followed Rafael to a nearby lounge, where he ordered a bottle of fine wine and invited Mia and Ivan to join him. The atmosphere was relaxed, and Rafael seemed eager to share his passion for art and history.

"Tell me more about your interest in these paintings," Mia said, her voice warm and engaging.

Rafael leaned back, swirling his wine glass thoughtfully. "The paintings are part of a larger narrative, one that spans centuries. They're connected to a secret society that protected valuable artifacts and knowledge. I've been collecting pieces of this puzzle for years, and these paintings are a crucial part of it."

Mia and Ivan exchanged a glance, their curiosity piqued. "That's fascinating. Do you have any leads on where this knowledge might be hidden?" Ivan asked, his tone casual.

Rafael hesitated, then smiled. "I've uncovered several clues, but the final piece of the puzzle is still missing. There's a legend about a hidden chamber in an ancient library, where the society's most valuable secrets were kept. I believe these paintings contain the key to finding it."

Mia's mind raced. The hidden chamber could be the final piece of their investigation, the place where the full story of the artifact and the secret society was revealed. "Do you have any idea where this library might be?" she asked, her voice tinged with excitement.

Rafael nodded. "I have a few leads. The library is said to be located in an old monastery, not far from here. It's been abandoned for centuries, but I believe it holds the answers we seek."

Mia felt a surge of anticipation. They were closer than ever to uncovering the full story. "We should explore it together. Combining our knowledge could help us unlock its secrets."

Rafael agreed, and they made plans to visit the monastery the next day. As Mia and Ivan left the lounge, they felt a renewed sense of purpose. They were on the brink of a major breakthrough, one that could change the course of their investigation.

That night, as Mia lay in bed, she felt a mix of excitement and trepidation. The journey had been long and dangerous, but they were finally closing in on the truth. With Ivan by her side, she felt ready to face whatever challenges lay ahead.

Sleep came slowly, her dreams filled with swirling patterns, hidden messages, and the boundless possibilities of her art and her future. The journey was nearing its climax, and she was ready to embrace the next chapter with open arms and an open heart.

Chapter 18: A Secret Meeting

The first light of dawn filtered through the curtains, casting a gentle glow over the room. Mia awoke with a sense of anticipation, knowing that today could bring them closer to uncovering the full story behind the artifact and the hidden messages in the paintings. After a quick breakfast, she met Ivan in the hotel lobby. His expression mirrored her own excitement and determination.

"Morning, Mia. Ready for today's adventure?" Ivan greeted her with a warm smile.

"Absolutely. This could be the breakthrough we've been waiting for," Mia replied, her eyes sparkling with resolve.

They had arranged to meet Rafael at the old monastery he had mentioned the previous night. The drive through the countryside was filled with a mix of anticipation and tension, both of them keenly aware of the potential dangers but eager to uncover the truth.

The monastery was an imposing structure, its ancient stone walls weathered by time. It stood on a secluded hill, surrounded by dense forest. As they approached, Mia felt a chill run down her spine. The place seemed to hold secrets, its silence almost palpable.

Rafael was waiting for them at the entrance, his expression serious but welcoming. "Good morning. I'm glad you could make it. This place holds many secrets, and I believe we can unlock them together."

"Thank you for including us, Rafael. We're eager to see what we can find," Mia said, shaking his hand.

They entered the monastery, the air cool and damp. The interior was dimly lit, with long shadows cast by the narrow windows. Rafael led them through a series of winding corridors, their footsteps echoing softly in the silence.

"This monastery was once a place of great learning and wisdom," Rafael explained as they walked. "It housed a vast library, and according to legend, a hidden chamber where the society's most valuable secrets were kept."

Mia and Ivan listened intently, their eyes scanning the ancient walls for any clues. They reached a large room filled with dusty books and crumbling scrolls, the remnants of the once-great library. Rafael motioned for them to stop.

"This is where the legend says the entrance to the hidden chamber is located," Rafael said, his voice hushed with reverence. "We need to find a specific set of symbols that will reveal the way."

They began to search the room, examining the walls, shelves, and floors for any signs of the symbols. Mia's heart raced with excitement and anticipation. After what felt like hours, Ivan called out.

"Over here! I think I found something."

Mia and Rafael hurried over to where Ivan was standing. He had discovered a set of symbols etched into the stone floor, barely visible under layers of dust and grime. They matched the symbols in the paintings and the manuscript they had studied.

"This is it," Rafael said, his voice filled with awe. "We need to follow these symbols. They should lead us to the hidden chamber."

They carefully traced the symbols, which formed a path through the library. The trail led them to a large, ornate bookshelf. Mia felt a surge of anticipation as she examined the shelf, looking for any hidden mechanisms.

"There must be a way to move this," Mia said, her fingers running over the intricate carvings.

Ivan found a small, concealed latch and pressed it. With a soft click, the bookshelf began to move, revealing a hidden doorway behind it. Mia's heart raced as they stepped through the doorway into a narrow, dimly lit corridor.

The corridor led to a small, hidden chamber. Inside, they found a treasure trove of ancient artifacts, scrolls, and manuscripts. Mia felt a sense of awe and reverence as she realized the significance of their discovery.

"This is incredible," Ivan said, his voice filled with wonder. "We've found the hidden chamber."

Rafael's eyes shone with excitement. "These artifacts and manuscripts hold the secrets of the society. We need to study them carefully."

They spent the next few hours examining the contents of the chamber. The manuscripts detailed the history of the secret society, its purpose, and the measures they had taken to protect their knowledge. The artifacts included ancient tools, symbols, and a small, intricately carved box.

Mia carefully opened the box, revealing a collection of finely crafted keys and a detailed map. The map seemed to indicate the locations of other hidden chambers and artifacts, each one connected to the society's history and mission.

"This map could lead us to even more discoveries," Mia said, her voice filled with excitement. "We need to follow these leads."

As they continued to study the contents of the chamber, they heard a noise from outside. Mia's heart skipped a beat as she realized they were not alone. They quickly hid the artifacts and manuscripts, ready to confront whoever was approaching.

The door to the chamber creaked open, and a figure stepped inside. It was one of Isabella's associates, his expression filled with malice and determination. He was followed by two more men, their intentions clear.

"Well, well, what do we have here?" the leader sneered. "Looks like you've found something valuable. Hand it over, and no one gets hurt."

Mia felt a surge of fear but stood her ground. "We're not giving you anything. These artifacts belong to the world, not to those who would misuse them."

The man's expression darkened. "I don't think you understand. We're not asking."

Before Mia could react, the men lunged at them. Ivan stepped forward, his fists raised in defense. A struggle ensued, the confined space of the chamber making it difficult to move. Mia clutched the box to her chest, her heart racing.

Rafael, though not a fighter, grabbed a nearby object and swung it at one of the men, buying Ivan a moment to gain the upper hand. With a swift movement, Ivan knocked one of the attackers to the ground, but the other two were still advancing.

"We need to get out of here!" Mia shouted, her voice filled with urgency.

Using their combined strength, they managed to push past the attackers and make a break for the exit. The dark corridors of the monastery seemed to stretch endlessly, but they kept running, fueled by adrenaline and fear.

As they burst out into the open air, Mia felt a sense of relief, but she knew they weren't safe yet. They sprinted to their car, Ivan quickly starting the engine and speeding away from the monastery. Mia glanced back, her heart still pounding.

"That was too close," she said, her voice trembling with relief.

Ivan nodded, his expression serious. "We need to get these artifacts to Inspector Ruiz immediately. This information is too important to fall into the wrong hands."

The drive back to Sevilla was tense, both of them on high alert for any signs of danger. When they arrived at the police station, they were greeted by a surprised but relieved Inspector Ruiz.

"Mia, Ivan, what happened?" he asked, his eyes wide with concern.

"We found the hidden chamber," Mia said, holding up the small, intricately carved box. "But we were ambushed by Isabella's associates. We need to make sure these artifacts are kept safe."

Ruiz's expression hardened. "You did well. We'll ensure the artifacts are protected and that those responsible are brought to justice."

As they handed over the artifacts and the manuscripts, Mia felt a sense of accomplishment and relief. They had faced great danger, but they had succeeded in their mission. The artifacts were safe, and Isabella's network was being dismantled.

That night, as Mia lay in bed, she felt a mix of exhaustion and contentment. The journey had been long and perilous, but they had uncovered the truth and brought justice for Alejandro. With Ivan by her side, she felt ready to face whatever challenges lay ahead.

Sleep came slowly, her dreams filled with swirling patterns, hidden messages, and the boundless possibilities of her art and her future. The journey had reached a critical point, and she was ready to embrace the next chapter with open arms and an open heart.

Chapter 19: Love and Loss

The morning sun rose over Sevilla, casting a soft, golden light over the city. Mia woke with a sense of both accomplishment and lingering tension from the previous day's events. They had succeeded in securing the artifacts, but the danger of Isabella's network still loomed over them. Today, however, she was determined to take a moment to breathe and reflect on everything that had happened.

After a quick breakfast, Mia met Ivan in the hotel lobby. He greeted her with a warm smile and a gentle kiss on the cheek. "Morning, Mia. How are you feeling?"

"A bit tired, but relieved," Mia replied, her eyes showing a mix of exhaustion and contentment. "We've come so far, but I think we need to take a moment to appreciate what we've accomplished."

Ivan nodded in agreement. "I couldn't agree more. How about we spend the day exploring the city and enjoying ourselves for a change?"

Mia's eyes lit up at the suggestion. "That sounds perfect. I could use a break from all the intensity."

They decided to spend the day exploring the historic streets of Sevilla, immersing themselves in the city's vibrant culture. They visited the stunning Alcázar, strolled through the fragrant gardens of Maria Luisa Park, and enjoyed the lively atmosphere of Plaza de España. As they wandered through the city, Mia felt a sense of peace and rejuvenation. The beauty of Sevilla provided a much-needed respite from the chaos of their investigation.

Around midday, they found a charming café in a quiet corner of the city. They settled into a cozy table outside, enjoying the warm sunshine and the delicious aroma of freshly brewed coffee. As they sipped their drinks, Mia felt a deep connection with Ivan, one that had grown stronger through their shared experiences.

"Ivan, I'm so grateful for everything you've done," Mia said, her voice filled with emotion. "I couldn't have done any of this without you."

Ivan reached across the table and took her hand, his eyes filled with warmth. "Mia, it's been an incredible journey, and I'm glad we've faced it together. You've inspired me in so many ways."

Mia felt a warmth spread through her chest. "I feel the same way. You've been my rock through all of this."

As they talked, their conversation drifted to lighter topics, their laughter mingling with the sounds of the bustling city around them. Mia felt a sense of contentment that she hadn't experienced in a long time. For a moment, the weight of their mission lifted, and they were just two people enjoying each other's company.

After their leisurely lunch, they continued their exploration of the city, visiting art galleries and local shops. Mia found herself inspired by the vibrant art scene of Sevilla, her mind buzzing with ideas for new projects. Ivan captured moments with his camera, his keen eye for detail bringing the city's beauty to life.

As the sun began to set, they made their way to a small, picturesque plaza. The air was filled with the sound of a nearby flamenco performance, the passionate music and dance creating an enchanting atmosphere. They found a bench and sat down, enjoying the performance and the beauty of the evening.

Mia leaned her head on Ivan's shoulder, feeling a sense of peace. "This has been a perfect day."

"It really has," Ivan replied, his arm wrapping around her. "I think we needed this."

They sat in comfortable silence, the music washing over them. Mia felt a deep sense of gratitude for Ivan and the journey they had shared. She knew that their mission was far from over, but for now, she allowed herself to savor the moment.

As the night fell, they made their way back to the hotel. The streets of Sevilla were illuminated by the soft glow of streetlights, creating a magical ambiance. Mia felt a sense of anticipation and excitement for the future, knowing that with Ivan by her side, they could face any challenge.

Back in their room, Mia and Ivan shared a quiet dinner, their conversation filled with dreams and plans for the future. They spoke about their art, their hopes, and the projects they wanted to pursue together. Mia felt a deep connection with Ivan, one that transcended their shared experiences.

After dinner, they moved to the balcony, the city's lights twinkling below them. Ivan pulled Mia close, his eyes reflecting the love and admiration he felt for her. "Mia, you mean so much to me. This journey has been incredible, and I can't imagine doing it without you."

Mia felt tears of happiness well up in her eyes. "Ivan, I feel the same way. You've been my strength, my inspiration. I love you."

Ivan leaned in and kissed her softly, their connection deepening with every moment. They stood there, wrapped in each other's arms, the world around them fading away.

As they eventually moved back inside, the atmosphere between them grew more intimate. They shared a tender, passionate moment, their connection intensifying. The love they felt for each other was palpable, and though they avoided taking it to the next level, the depth of their bond was undeniable.

That night, as Mia lay in bed with Ivan by her side, she felt a sense of contentment and hope. The journey had been long and challenging, but they had faced it together and emerged stronger. With Ivan's love and support, she knew they could conquer whatever lay ahead.

Sleep came slowly, her dreams filled with swirling patterns, hidden messages, and the boundless possibilities of her art and her future with Ivan. The journey had brought them closer than ever, and she was ready to embrace the next chapter with open arms and an open heart.

Chapter 20: The Reveal

The morning light filtered through the curtains, casting a gentle glow over the room. Mia awoke with a sense of purpose, feeling the warmth of Ivan beside her. The previous day had been a welcome respite, but now it was time to return to their mission. She got out of bed quietly, not wanting to disturb Ivan, and made her way to the balcony to gather her thoughts.

As she stood there, looking out over the city, Mia felt a surge of determination. They had come so far, uncovered so much, and now they were on the brink of a major breakthrough. She knew that today could be the day they finally uncovered the full extent of Isabella's network.

A few minutes later, Ivan joined her on the balcony, wrapping his arms around her from behind. "Good morning, Mia. Ready to take on the world?"

Mia smiled, leaning back into his embrace. "Good morning, Ivan. Yes, I'm ready. We have so much to do, but I feel like we're so close to uncovering everything."

They shared a quick breakfast and then headed to the police station to meet with Inspector Ruiz. He greeted them with a nod, his expression serious. "Good morning. I've been reviewing the artifacts and manuscripts you found. They're extraordinary, but we need to connect the final dots to bring Isabella's entire operation down."

Mia and Ivan explained their plan to Ruiz. They believed that the hidden messages in the paintings, combined with the new artifacts, could lead them to critical evidence. They needed to analyze everything one more time to ensure they hadn't missed anything.

"We need to go back to Luis's studio and take another look at those paintings," Mia said. "I have a feeling we're missing something important."

Ruiz agreed, and they headed to the studio. Luis welcomed them warmly, eager to continue their investigation. They spread out the photographs, manuscripts, and artifacts on the large table, carefully examining each piece for any clues.

As they worked, Mia's mind raced. The symbols, patterns, and hidden messages had led them this far, but there was still a piece of the puzzle missing. She felt a growing sense of frustration, knowing that they were so close yet still searching for the final connection.

Suddenly, Ivan's eyes widened as he looked at one of the photographs under a different light. "Mia, look at this. I think I've found something."

Mia hurried over, her heart pounding with anticipation. Ivan pointed to a faint symbol that had appeared in the photograph under the ultraviolet light. It was a symbol they hadn't noticed before, hidden beneath layers of paint.

"This symbol matches one of the artifacts we found in the hidden chamber," Mia said, her voice filled with excitement. "It's part of the key to deciphering the final message."

They carefully compared the symbol with the artifacts and manuscripts, slowly piecing together the hidden message. It was a map, leading to a location that had been obscured in the paintings. The map pointed to an abandoned warehouse on the outskirts of Sevilla, a place they hadn't considered before.

"This is it," Mia said, her voice trembling with excitement. "The final piece of the puzzle. We need to go there and see what we can find."

With renewed determination, they packed up their findings and set off for the warehouse. The drive was filled with a mix of anticipation and tension, both of them keenly aware of the potential dangers but eager to uncover the truth.

The warehouse was a large, imposing structure, its exterior weathered and overgrown with vines. As they approached, Mia felt a chill run down her spine. The place seemed abandoned, but she knew better than to let her guard down.

They carefully made their way inside, the interior dimly lit and filled with shadows. The air was cool and damp, the silence almost oppressive. Mia's heart pounded in her chest as they followed the map's directions, moving deeper into the building.

"This place gives me the creeps," Ivan whispered, his eyes scanning the darkness.

"Stay close," Mia replied, her voice steady. "We're almost there."

They reached a large room at the back of the warehouse, its walls lined with old crates and forgotten machinery. In the center of the room, they found a large, ornate chest, covered in dust and cobwebs. Mia's heart raced as she approached the chest, her hands trembling with anticipation.

"This must be it," she whispered, carefully opening the lid.

Inside, they found a collection of documents, photographs, and ledgers. Mia felt a surge of triumph as she realized what they had uncovered. The documents detailed the full extent of Isabella's network, including names, dates, and transactions. It was the evidence they needed to bring her entire operation down.

"We did it," Ivan said, his voice filled with awe. "This is everything we've been looking for."

Mia felt tears of relief and joy well up in her eyes. "We need to get this to Inspector Ruiz immediately. This will bring Isabella to justice."

As they carefully packed up the evidence, Mia couldn't shake the feeling that they were being watched. She glanced around the room, her senses on high alert. Suddenly, the sound of footsteps echoed through the warehouse.

"Get down!" Ivan shouted, pulling Mia behind a stack of crates.

They crouched in the shadows, their hearts pounding as the footsteps grew closer. Mia held her breath, praying they wouldn't be discovered. After what felt like an eternity, the footsteps receded, and the warehouse fell silent once more.

"We need to get out of here," Mia whispered, her voice trembling.

Ivan nodded, and they quickly made their way back to the entrance, their senses on high alert. They reached their car and sped away from the warehouse, the tension in the air palpable.

When they arrived at the police station, they were greeted by a surprised but relieved Inspector Ruiz. "Mia, Ivan, what happened? Did you find anything?"

"We found everything," Mia said, holding up the documents. "This is the evidence we need to bring Isabella's entire network down."

Ruiz's eyes widened as he examined the documents, understanding the significance of their discovery. "This is incredible. With this evidence, we can finally put an end to Isabella's operation."

Mia and Ivan felt a wave of relief and satisfaction. They had faced great danger, but they had succeeded in their mission. Isabella's network would be dismantled, and justice would be served.

That night, as Mia lay in bed with Ivan by her side, she felt a sense of contentment and hope. The journey had been long and challenging, but they had uncovered the truth and brought justice for Alejandro. With Ivan's love and support, she felt ready to face whatever challenges lay ahead.

Sleep came slowly, her dreams filled with swirling patterns, hidden messages, and the boundless possibilities of her art and her future with Ivan. The journey had reached a new chapter, and she was ready to embrace it with open arms and an open heart.

Chapter 21: Confrontation

The morning dawned crisp and clear over Sevilla, but the atmosphere inside the police station was tense. Mia, Ivan, and Inspector Ruiz gathered around a table piled high with documents and evidence from their recent discoveries. The weight of their findings hung heavy in the air as they prepared to confront Isabella and her network.

"Mia, Ivan, what you've uncovered is remarkable," Inspector Ruiz began, his voice serious. "We have enough evidence here to dismantle Isabella's entire operation. But we need to proceed carefully."

Mia nodded, her expression determined. "We understand, Inspector. Isabella won't go down without a fight, but we're prepared."

Ruiz glanced at the stack of documents, each page representing years of illegal transactions and manipulation within the art world. "We'll coordinate with other law enforcement agencies to ensure a comprehensive approach. Isabella has connections, but with this evidence, we have the upper hand."

Ivan tapped his fingers on the table, his mind racing with the implications of their discovery. "What's our next move, Inspector?"

"We need to set up a sting operation," Ruiz replied, flipping through the evidence. "Isabella and her associates must be apprehended simultaneously to prevent any escape or destruction of evidence."

Mia leaned forward, her eyes narrowing with determination. "We can use the paintings and artifacts as bait. They'll think we're still searching for clues while we move in to arrest them."

Ruiz nodded in agreement. "Exactly. We'll coordinate with undercover agents to monitor their movements. Once we have confirmation of their location, we strike."

As they finalized their plan, Mia couldn't shake the feeling of unease. Isabella was a formidable opponent, and they were about to confront her head-on. But she drew strength from Ivan's steady presence and Ruiz's unwavering resolve.

Several tense hours passed as they coordinated with the undercover agents and prepared for the operation. Mia and Ivan returned to their hotel briefly to gather their belongings and steel themselves for the confrontation ahead.

"Ivan, are you sure you're ready for this?" Mia asked quietly as they packed.

He turned to her with a reassuring smile. "I'm with you every step of the way, Mia. We've come too far to turn back now."

She nodded, grateful for his support. "I know. It's just... this is our chance to finally bring justice for Alejandro and put an end to Isabella's schemes."

They arrived at the designated meeting point near the outskirts of Sevilla, where Ruiz and his team were already in position. Undercover agents blended into the surroundings, their eyes trained on the warehouse where Isabella and her associates were expected to gather.

Mia felt a surge of adrenaline as they waited in tense anticipation. The sun began to set, casting long shadows across the abandoned warehouse and surrounding area. Every minute felt like an eternity as they maintained vigilance, ready to move at a moment's notice.

Suddenly, Ruiz's voice crackled over the radio. "They're on the move. Get ready."

Mia and Ivan exchanged a quick glance before following Ruiz and his team toward the warehouse. They moved swiftly and silently, their senses on high alert. The air was charged with anticipation as they approached the building.

In the dim light of dusk, they saw figures moving inside the warehouse. Isabella and her associates were gathered around a table, examining paintings and discussing their next moves. Mia's jaw tightened as she recognized Isabella's cold demeanor and calculating gaze.

Ruiz signaled for his team to move in. Mia and Ivan stayed close behind, ready to provide support if needed. The undercover agents surrounded the warehouse, closing in on Isabella and her associates from all sides.

"Police! Freeze!" Ruiz's voice boomed through the warehouse as his team burst through the doors.

Isabella's eyes widened in shock as she realized she had been caught. Her associates tried to flee, but they were quickly apprehended by the waiting agents. Mia felt a mix of satisfaction and relief as justice finally caught up with them.

"You've got nothing on me!" Isabella spat defiantly as she was handcuffed.

Ruiz approached her calmly, holding up the stack of incriminating documents. "On the contrary, Isabella. We have everything we need to put you away for a long time."

As Isabella was led away, Mia and Ivan exchanged a quiet sigh of relief. They had succeeded in their mission, bringing closure to Alejandro's murder and dismantling Isabella's criminal network. The weight that had been hanging over them for so long finally lifted.

Back at the police station, Ruiz congratulated Mia and Ivan on their bravery and perseverance. "You two have done an outstanding job. Sevilla owes you a debt of gratitude."

Mia smiled gratefully, but her thoughts were already turning to the future. With Isabella behind bars, she felt a sense of freedom and possibility. She knew there were new challenges and adventures waiting for her, both in her art and in her relationship with Ivan.

That night, as they celebrated their victory with a quiet dinner, Mia couldn't help but feel a sense of pride. They had faced danger and uncertainty together, and they had emerged stronger than ever. With Ivan by her side, she knew they could face anything that came their way.

As they toasted to the future, Mia felt a sense of excitement for what lay ahead. The journey had been long and challenging, but it had also been filled with moments of joy, discovery, and love. With their bond stronger than ever, she knew they were ready to embrace whatever came next.

Sleep came easily that night, her dreams filled with visions of vibrant colors, swirling patterns, and the endless possibilities of her art and her future with Ivan. The journey had brought them together in ways she had never imagined, and she was ready to see where their next adventure would take them.

The End

Don't miss out!

Visit the website below and you can sign up to receive emails whenever Adela Vesper publishes a new book. There's no charge and no obligation.

https://books2read.com/r/B-A-VQLJB-ADDOD

BOOKS 2 READ

Connecting independent readers to independent writers.

Did you love *SHADOWS OF SEVILLE An Artistic Mystery Romance*? Then you should read *Palette of Intrigue - A Female-Led Mystery Unveiling Barcelona Art Scene*[1] by Adela Vesper!

[2]

Step into the alluring world of Barcelona's bustling art scene, where every stroke of paint conceals a secret, and every masterpiece holds a story untold. In 'A Female-Led Mystery Unveiling Barcelona Art Scene,' embark on a thrilling journey alongside Mia, a talented abstract painter whose brushwork uncovers more than just beauty. When a daring art heist rocks the city's cultural landscape, Mia finds herself thrust into the heart of the investigation, her keen eye for detail and unwavering determination propelling her forward.

As Mia delves deeper into the shadows of Barcelona's galleries and museums, she discovers a labyrinth of deceit, betrayal, and intrigue.

1. https://books2read.com/u/4XjkY9

2. https://books2read.com/u/4XjkY9

With each clue she uncovers, the mystery deepens, leading her down twisting paths of art forgery, smuggling, and high-stakes crime. But Mia is not alone in her quest for the truth; alongside her stands a cast of colorful characters, each with their own motives and secrets to unravel.

From the sun-drenched streets of La Rambla to the hidden corners of the Gothic Quarter, Mia races against time to unravel the threads of deception before they unravel her. But as she inches closer to the heart of the mystery, Mia realizes that the true challenge lies not in solving the crime, but in confronting the demons of her own past.

In this gripping tale of suspense, discovery, and redemption, 'A Female-Led Mystery Unveiling Barcelona Art Scene' invites readers on an unforgettable journey through the intersection of art and intrigue. With its richly drawn characters, evocative setting, and pulse-pounding plot, this is a novel that will keep you on the edge of your seat until the very last page

Also by Adela Vesper

Palette of Intrigue - A Female-Led Mystery Unveiling Barcelona Art Scene
Echoes of Wycliffe : A Legacy Restored
The Lady's Secret : A Regency Affair
SHADOWS OF SEVILLE An Artistic Mystery Romance